That night, when all was still, White Fang remembered his mother and cried sorrowfully for her.

He wept too loudly and woke up Gray Beaver, who beat him. After that he mourned gently when the gods were around. But sometimes, straying off to the edge of the woods by himself, he wailed out his grief loudly. During this time, he might have run back to the Wild, but the memory of his mother held him. After all, the hunting man-animals went out and came back. She, too, might return someday, so he remained in bondage and waited for her.

JACK LONDON

White Fang

Edited by Jonathan Kelley

Afterword by Beth Johnson

 **THE TOWNSEND LIBRARY**

WHITE FANG

TP THE TOWNSEND LIBRARY

For more titles in the Townsend Library,
visit our website: **www.townsendpress.com**

Townsend Press, Inc.
1038 Industrial Drive
West Berlin, New Jersey 08091

ISBN 1-59194-007-9

Library of Congress Control Number:
2003100035

TABLE OF CONTENTS

PART ONE:
THE WILD

CHAPTER 1

The Trail of the Meat

Dark spruce forest frowned on either side of the frozen waterway. The trees seemed to lean toward each other, black and ominous in the fading light. A vast silence reigned over the desolate, lifeless land. The land was so lone and cold that its spirit was not even that of sadness, but one which held a hint of laughter as cold as the frost. It was the all-powerful wisdom of eternity laughing at the futility of life. It was the Wild—the savage, frozen-hearted Northland Wild.

But there was life, abroad in the land and defiant. Down the frozen waterway toiled a string of wolfish dogs, their bristly fur coated with frost. Their breath froze as it left their mouths. Leather harnesses were on the dogs, and leather traces attached them to a birch-bark sled which dragged along behind. The sled was without runners. On the sled, securely lashed, was a long and narrow oblong box. There were other things on the sled—blankets, an axe, and a coffeepot and frying pan; but prominent, occupying most of the space, was the long and narrow oblong box.

Ahead of the dogs, on wide snowshoes, toiled a man. Behind the sled toiled a second man. On the sled, in the box, lay a third man whose toil was over—a man whom the Wild had conquered and beaten down, never to move or struggle again. Life offends the Wild—for life is movement. The Wild aims always to destroy all movement. It freezes the water to prevent it from running to the sea, it drives the sap out of the trees till they are frozen to their mighty hearts, and most ferociously and terribly of all, it crushes man into submission.

But at the front and the rear, the two men toiled on, unawed and indomitable. Their bodies were covered with fur and soft-tanned leather. Eyelashes and cheeks and lips were so coated with the crystals from their frozen breath that their faces were obscured. This gave them a masked look, like undertakers at a ghostly funeral. But under it all they were men, penetrating the desolation and silence, puny adventurers bent on colossal adventure, pitting themselves against the might of a

remote, alien world.

They traveled on without speech, saving their breath for the work of their bodies. On every side was the silence, pressing in on their minds as deep water does to a diver's body, until they felt finite and small and naïve amidst the interplay of the great elements.

An hour went by, and then another. The pale light of the short sunless day was fading when a faint, far cry arose on the still air. It soared upward with a swift rush, peaked, then slowly died away. It might have been a lost soul wailing, had it not been invested with a certain sad fierceness and hungry eagerness. The front man turned to meet the eyes of the man behind. Across the oblong box, each nodded to the other.

A second cry arose, piercing the silence like a needle. Both men located the sound. It was to the rear, somewhere in the snowy expanse they had just crossed. A third and answering cry arose, also behind and to the left of the second cry.

"They're after us, Bill," said the man at the front, his voice labored and hoarse.

"Meat is scarce," answered his comrade. "I ain't seen sign of a rabbit for days."

They spoke no more, but listened keenly for the hunting-cries that continued to rise behind them.

At the fall of darkness, they swung the dogs into a cluster of spruce trees on the edge of the waterway and made a camp. The coffin served as seat and table. The wolfish sled-dogs, clustered on the far side of the fire, snarled and bickered among themselves, but showed no inclination to stray off into the darkness.

"Seems to me, Henry, they're stayin' remarkable close to camp," Bill commented.

Henry, squatting over the fire and settling the pot of coffee with a piece of ice, nodded. He kept silent until he was seated on the coffin, eating.

"They know where their hides is safe," he said. "They'd sooner eat grub than be grub. They're pretty wise, them dogs."

Bill shook his head. "Oh, I don't know."

His comrade looked at him curiously. "First time I ever heard you say anything about their not bein' wise."

"Henry," said the other, munching his beans with deliberation, "did you happen to notice the way them dogs kicked up when I was a-feedin' 'em?"

"They did cut up more'n usual," Henry acknowledged.

"How many dogs've we got, Henry?"

"Six."

"Well, Henry . . . " Bill stopped a moment for emphasis. "As I was sayin', Henry, we've got six dogs. I took six fish out of the bag. I gave one fish to each dog, an', Henry, I was one fish short."

"You counted wrong."

"We've got six dogs," the other repeated dispassionately. "I took out six fish. One Ear didn't get no fish. I came back to the bag afterward an' got 'm his fish."

"We've only got six dogs," Henry said.

"Henry," Bill went on. "I won't say they was all dogs, but there was seven of 'm that got fish."

Henry stopped eating to glance across the fire and count the dogs. "There's only six now," he said.

"I saw the other one run off across the snow," Bill announced positively. "I saw seven."

Henry looked at him in sympathy, and said, "I'll be almighty glad when this trip's over."

"What d'ye mean by that?" Bill demanded.

"I mean that this load of ours is gettin' on your nerves, an' that you're beginnin' to see things."

"I thought of that," Bill answered gravely.

"An' so, when I saw it run off across the snow, I looked in the snow an' saw its tracks. Then I counted the dogs an' there was still six of 'em. The tracks is there in the snow now. D'ye want to look at 'em? I'll show 'em to you."

Henry finished eating in silence, topping the meal with a final cup of coffee. He wiped his mouth with the back of his hand and finally replied: "Then you're thinkin' as it was—"

A long, fiercely sad wail interrupted him from somewhere in the darkness. He stopped to listen to it; then he finished his sentence with a wave of his hand toward the sound of the cry—". . . one of them?"

Bill nodded. "I'd sooner think that than anything else. You yourself noticed the row the dogs made."

Cry after cry, and answering cries were turning the silence into bedlam. The cries arose from every side. The dogs huddled together in fear, so close to the fire that the heat scorched their hair. Bill threw on more wood before lighting his pipe.

"I'm thinking you're down in the mouth some," Henry said.

"Henry . . . " He sucked meditatively at his pipe for some time before he went on. "Henry, I was a-thinkin' what a blame sight luckier he is than you an' me'll ever be." He pointed to the coffin on which they sat. "You an' me, Henry, when we die, we'll be lucky if we get enough stones over our carcasses to keep the dogs off of us."

"But we ain't got people an' money an' all the rest, like him," Henry rejoined. "Long-distance funerals is somethin' you an' me can't exactly afford."

"What gets me, Henry, is what a chap like this, that's a lord or something in his own country, and that's never had to bother about grub nor blankets, why he comes a-buttin' round the Godforsaken ends of the earth."

"He might have lived to a ripe old age if he'd stayed at home," Henry agreed.

Bill opened his mouth to speak, but changed his mind. Instead, he pointed toward the wall of darkness that pressed about them from every side. There was no suggestion of form in the utter blackness. All that could be seen was a pair of eyes gleaming like live coals in the darkness. Henry indicated with his head a second pair, and a third. A circle of the gleaming eyes had drawn about their camp. Now and again a pair of eyes moved, or disappeared and then reappeared a moment later.

The dogs' unrest had been increasing. They stampeded in a surge of sudden fear to the near side of the fire, cringing and crawling about the legs of the men. In the scramble one of the dogs was overturned on the edge of the fire. It yelped with pain and fright as the smell of its singed coat possessed the air. The commotion caused the circle of eyes to shift restlessly for a moment and even to withdraw a bit, but it settled down again as the dogs became quiet.

"Henry, it's a blame misfortune to be out of ammunition."

Bill had finished his pipe and was helping his companion to spread the bed of fur and blanket upon the spruce boughs which he had laid over the snow before supper. Henry grunted and began unlacing his moccasins.

"How many cartridges did you say you had left?" he asked.

"Three," came the answer. "An' I wisht 'twas three hundred. Then I'd show 'em what for, damn 'em!" He shook his fist angrily at the gleaming eyes and began to prop his moccasins before the fire.

"An' I wisht this cold snap'd break," he went on. "It's been fifty below for two weeks now. An' I wisht I'd never started on this trip, Henry. I don't like the looks of it. I don't feel right, somehow. An' while I'm wishin', I wisht the trip was over an' done with, an' you an' me a-sittin' by the fire in Fort McGurry just about now an' playing cribbage."

Henry grunted and crawled into bed. As he dozed off, he was reawakened by his comrade's voice.

"Say, Henry, that other one that come in an' got a fish—why didn't the dogs pitch into it? That's what's botherin' me."

"You're botherin' too much, Bill," came the sleepy response. "You was never like this before. You jes' shut up now, an' go to sleep, an' you'll be all hunkydory in the mornin'. Your stomach's sour, that's what's botherin' you."

The men slept, breathing heavily, side by side under the one covering. The fire died down, and the gleaming eyes tightened the circle they had flung about the camp. The dogs clustered together in fear, now and again snarling menacingly as a pair of eyes drew close. Once their uproar became so loud that Bill woke up. He got out of bed carefully, so as not to disturb the sleep of his comrade, and threw more wood on the fire. As it began to flame up, the circle of eyes drew farther back. He glanced casually at the huddling dogs, then rubbed his eyes and looked at them more sharply. Then he crawled back into the blankets.

"Henry," he said. "Oh, Henry."

Henry groaned as he passed from sleep to waking and demanded, "What's wrong now?"

"Nothin'," came the answer. "Only there's seven of 'em again. I just counted."

Henry acknowledged receipt of the information with a grunt that slid into a snore as he drifted back into sleep.

In the morning it was Henry who awoke first and got his companion out of bed. Daylight was yet three hours away, though it was already six o'clock. Henry went about preparing breakfast in the dark, while Bill rolled the blankets and made the sled ready for lashing.

"Say, Henry," he asked suddenly, "how many dogs did you say we had?"

"Six."

"Wrong," Bill proclaimed triumphantly.

"Seven again?" Henry queried.

"No, five; one's gone."

"The hell!" Henry cried in wrath, leaving the cooking to come and count the dogs.

"You're right, Bill," he concluded. "Fatty's gone."

"An' he went like greased lightnin' once he got started. Couldn't 've seen 'em for smoke."

"No chance at all," Henry concluded. "They jes' swallowed 'm alive. I bet he was yelpin' as he went down their throats, damn 'em!"

"He always was a fool dog," said Bill.

"But no fool dog ought to be fool enough to go off an' commit suicide that way." He looked over the team with a speculative eye that instantly summed up the key traits of each animal. "I bet none of the others would do it."

"Couldn't drive 'em away from the fire with a club," Bill agreed. "I always did think there was somethin' wrong with Fatty, anyway."

And this was the epitaph of many a dead dog on the Northland trail, and of many a man.

CHAPTER TWO
THE SHE-WOLF

Breakfast eaten, and the camp packed for travel, the men turned their backs on the cheery fire and launched out into the darkness. At once, the fiercely sad cries began to call to one another through the darkness and cold. Conversation ceased. Daylight came at nine o'clock. At midday, the southern sky warmed to rose-color, then swiftly faded to a gray daylight that lasted until three. This, too, faded, and the Arctic night descended upon the lone and silent land.

As darkness came on, the hunting-cries around them drew closer—so close that more than once they sent surges of fear through the toiling dogs, throwing them into short-lived panics.

At the conclusion of one such panic, when he and Henry had gotten the dogs reharnessed, Bill said, "I wisht they'd strike game somewheres, an' go away an' leave us alone."

"They do get on the nerves horrible," Henry sympathized. They spoke no more until camp was made.

Henry was bending over and adding ice to the babbling pot of beans when he was startled by the sound of a blow, an exclamation from

Bill, and a sharp, snarling cry of pain from among the dogs. He stood up in time to see a dim form vanish into the dark. Then he saw Bill, standing amid the dogs, half triumphant, half crestfallen, in one hand a stout club, in the other part of the body of a sun-cured salmon.

"It got half of it," he announced, "but I got a whack at it jes' the same. D'ye hear it squeal?"

"What'd it look like?" Henry asked.

"Couldn't see. But it had four legs an' a mouth an' hair an' looked like any dog."

"Must be a tame wolf, I reckon."

"It's damned tame, whatever it is, comin' in here at feedin' time an' gettin' its fish."

That night, when supper was finished and they sat on the oblong box smoking pipes, the circle of gleaming eyes drew in even closer than before.

"I wisht they'd stir up a bunch of moose or something, an' go away an' leave us alone," Bill said.

Henry grunted with fading sympathy. For a quarter of an hour they sat in silence. Henry stared at the fire, and Bill watched the circle of eyes that burned in the darkness just beyond the firelight.

"I wisht we was pullin' into McGurry

right now," he began again.

"Shut up your wishin' and your croakin'," Henry burst out angrily. "Your stomach's sour. Swallow a spoonful of bakin' soda, an' you'll be more pleasant company."

In the morning, Henry was aroused by Bill's cursing. He propped himself up on an elbow and saw his comrade standing among the dogs, looking frustrated and angry, his face distorted with passion.

"Hello!" Henry called. "What's up now?"

"Frog's gone," came the answer.

"No."

"I tell you, 'yes.'"

Henry leaped out of the blankets and over to the dogs. He counted them with care, then joined his partner in cursing the power of the Wild that had robbed them of another dog.

"Frog was the strongest dog of the bunch," Bill pronounced finally.

"An' he was no fool dog, neither," Henry added.

And so was recorded the second epitaph in two days.

They ate a gloomy breakfast and harnessed the four remaining dogs to the sled. The day was a repetition of the days that had gone before. The men toiled without speech across the face of the frozen world. The only sounds were the cries of their pursuers, ever closer as night began to fall. The dogs grew excited and frightened, causing fearful panics that tangled the traces and further depressed the men.

"There, that'll fix you fool critters," Bill said with satisfaction that night, standing erect after completing his task.

Henry left the cooking to come and see. Not only had his partner tied up the dogs, but he had tied them up Indian fashion. Each dog had a leather thong about its neck, closely attached to a stick four or five feet long. The other end of the stick was tied to a stake. This kept the dog from gnawing his way loose.

Henry nodded his head approvingly. "It's the only thing that'll ever hold One Ear," he said. "He can gnaw through leather as clean an' quick as a knife. They'll all be here in the mornin' hunkydory."

"You jes' bet they will," Bill affirmed. "If one of em' turns up missin', I'll go without my coffee."

"They jes' know we ain't loaded to kill," Henry remarked at bedtime, indicating the gleaming circle that hemmed them in. "If we could shoot a couple, they'd be more respectful. They come closer every night. Get the firelight out of your eyes an' look hard.

There! Did you see that one?"

For some time the two men amused themselves with watching the vague forms on the edge of the firelight. By looking closely and steadily at where a pair of eyes burned into the darkness, the form of an animal would slowly take shape. They could even see these forms move at times.

A sound among the dogs attracted the men's attention. One Ear was uttering quick, eager whines, straining at the length of his stick toward the darkness, and stopping now and again to attack it frantically with his teeth.

"Look at that, Bill," Henry whispered.

With a stealthy, sidelong movement, a doglike animal glided full into the firelight. It moved with mistrust and daring, cautiously observing the men, its attention fixed on the dogs. One Ear strained toward the intruder and whined eagerly.

"That fool One Ear don't seem scairt much," Bill said in a low tone.

"It's a she-wolf," Henry whispered back, "an' that accounts for Fatty an' Frog. She's the decoy. She draws out the dog, an' then the pack eats 'm up."

The fire crackled. A log fell apart with a loud sputtering noise. At the sound of it, the strange animal leaped back into the darkness.

"Henry, I'm a-thinkin' that that was the one I belted with the club."

"Ain't the slightest doubt in the world," was Henry's response.

"An' right here I want to remark," Bill went on, "that that animal's famil-yarity with campfires is suspicious an' immoral."

"It knows more'n a self-respectin' wolf ought to know," Henry agreed. "A wolf that knows to come in with the dogs at feedin' time has had experiences. That wolf's a dog, an' it's eaten a lot a' fish from the hand of man."

"An' if I get a chance, that wolf that's a dog'll be jes' meat," Bill declared. "We can't afford to lose no more animals."

"But you've only got three cartridges," Henry objected.

"I'll wait for a dead sure shot," was the reply.

In the morning, Henry renewed the fire and cooked, waking Bill only for breakfast. "You was sleepin' jes' too comfortable for anything," Henry told him. "I hadn't the heart to rouse you." Bill began to eat. He noticed that his cup was empty and started to reach for the coffee, but the pot was out of reach beside Henry.

"Say, Henry," he chided gently, "ain't you forgot somethin'?"

Henry looked about with great care and shook his head. Bill held up the empty cup.

"You don't get no coffee," Henry announced.

"Ain't run out?" Bill asked anxiously.

"Nope."

"You ain't thinkin' it'll hurt my digestion?"

"Nope."

Bill flushed angrily. "Then you explain yourself," he said.

"Spanker's gone," Henry answered.

With the air of one resigned to misfortune, Bill turned his head to count the dogs.

"How'd it happen?" he asked.

Henry shrugged his shoulders. "Don't know. Unless One Ear gnawed 'm loose. He couldn't a-done it himself, that's sure."

"The darned cuss." Bill spoke gravely, repressing his anger. "Jes' because he couldn't chew himself loose, he chews Spanker loose."

"Well, Spanker's troubles is over, anyway. I guess by this time he's digested in the bellies of twenty different wolves," was Henry's epitaph on the lost dog. "Have some coffee, Bill."

But Bill shook his head. "I'll be ding-dong-danged if I do. I said I wouldn't if a dog turned up missin', an' I won't."

"It's darn good coffee," Henry enticed. But Bill stubbornly ate a dry breakfast, washed down with mumbled curses at One Ear.

"I'll tie 'em up out of reach of each other tonight," Bill said, as they continued on the trail with Henry in front.

They had traveled little more than a hundred yards when Henry bent down and picked up something he recognized by touch. He flung it back so that it bounced off the sled and onto Bill's snowshoes.

"Mebbe you'll need that in your business," Henry said.

"It was the stick Spanker had been tied

with," Bill uttered with excitement.

"They ate 'em hide an' all," Bill announced. "The stick's as clean as a whistle. They've even ate the leather. They're damn hungry, Henry, an' they'll have you an' me wonderin' before this trip's over."

Henry laughed defiantly. "I ain't been trailed this way by wolves before, but I've gone through a whole lot worse an' kept my health. Takes more'n a handful of wolves to get to me, Bill, my son."

"I don't know," Bill muttered ominously. "I don't know."

"Well, you'll know all right when we pull into McGurry."

"I ain't feelin' special' enthusiastic," Bill persisted.

"You're ailin' . . . that's what's the matter with you," Henry diagnosed. "What you need is quinine, an' I'm goin' to dose you up soon's we get to McGurry."

Bill grunted his disagreement and lapsed into silence. The day was like all the other days. Light came at nine o'clock. At twelve o'clock the horizon was warmed by the unseen sun; and then began the cold gray of afternoon that would merge into night.

It was just after the sun's futile effort to appear that Bill slipped out the rifle and said,

"You keep goin', Henry. I'm goin' to hang back a moment."

"You'd better stick with the sled," his partner protested. "You've only got three cartridges, an' there's no tellin' what might happen."

"Who's croaking now?" Bill demanded triumphantly.

Henry made no reply, and plodded on alone, though often he cast anxious glances back into the gray solitude where he had left his partner. An hour later Bill caught up.

"They're scattered an' rangin' along wide," he said; "keeping up with us an' lookin' for game at the same time. You see, they're sure of us if they wait. In the meantime, they're pickin' up anything eatable that comes handy."

"They *think* they're sure of us," Henry corrected.

Bill ignored him. "I seen some of them. They're starved. They ain't had a bite to eat in weeks, I reckon, outside of Fatty an' Frog an' Spanker. Their ribs is showin', an' their stomachs is right up against their backbones. They're pretty desperate, I can tell you. They'll be goin' mad in a while, an' then watch out."

A few minutes later, Henry emitted a low,

warning whistle from behind the sled. Bill turned and looked, then quietly stopped the dogs. To the rear, in plain view, trotted a furry, slinking form. Its nose was to the trail, and it trotted with a peculiar, sliding, effortless gait. It halted when they did, regarding them steadily with nostrils that twitched as it studied their scent.

"It's the she-wolf," Bill answered.

The dogs had laid down in the snow, and Bill joined his partner at the sled. Together they watched the strange animal that had pursued them for days, destroying half their dogteam.

After a searching scrutiny, the animal trotted forward a few steps. It repeated this several times until it was a short hundred yards away. It paused, head up, and with sight and scent studied the two men. It looked at them in a strangely wistful way, in the manner of a dog. But its wistfulness was bred of hunger, as cruel as its own fangs, as merciless as the frost itself. It was large for a wolf, among the largest of its kind.

"Stands pretty close to two feet an' a half at the shoulders," Henry commented. "An' I'll bet it ain't far from five feet long."

"Kind of strange color for a wolf," Bill criticized. "I never seen a red wolf before.

Looks almost cinnamon to me."

The animal was certainly not cinnamon-colored. Its coat was the true wolf-coat: mostly gray, with a faint and baffling reddish hue.

"Looks for all the world like a big sled-dog," Bill said. "I wouldn't be s'prised to see it wag its tail. Hello, you husky!" he called. "Come here, you whatever-your-name-is."

"Ain't a bit scairt of you," Henry laughed.

Bill waved his hand at it, shouting threateningly. The animal showed no fear. It only became slightly more alert, still regarding them with the merciless wistfulness of hunger. They were meat, and it was hungry enough to eat them if it dared try.

"Look here, Henry," Bill whispered. "We've got three cartridges, but it's a dead shot. It's got away with three of our dogs, an' we oughter put a stop to it. What d'ye say?"

Henry nodded. Bill cautiously eased the gun out and toward his shoulder. Instantly the she-wolf leaped sidewise from the trail and disappeared into the spruce trees.

The two men looked at each other. Henry whistled comprehendingly.

"I might have knowed it," Bill said, as he replaced the gun. "Of course, a wolf that knows about dogs' feedin' time'd know all about shooting-irons. I tell you right now, Henry, that critter's the cause of all our trouble. We'd have six dogs now, 'stead of three, if it wasn't for her. An' I tell you right now, Henry, I'm goin' to get her. I'll bushwhack her as sure as my name is Bill."

"Don't stray off too far in doin' it," his partner admonished. "If that pack ever starts to jump you, that gun'd be wuthless. Them animals is damn hungry, an' once they start in, they'll sure get you, Bill."

Three dogs could not do the work of six, so they camped early that night. Bill tied the dogs out of gnawing-reach of one another, and they went to bed early. But the wolves were growing bolder, and the men were aroused more than once from their sleep. The dogs became frantic with terror, forcing the men to replenish the fire to keep the marauders at a distance.

"I've heard sailors talk of sharks followin' a ship," Bill remarked during one such arousal. "Well, them wolves is land sharks. They know their business better'n we do, an' they ain't a-trailin' us this way for their health. They're goin' to get us for sure, Henry."

"They've half got you a'ready, a-talkin' like that," Henry retorted sharply. "A man's half-licked when he says he is. An' you're half-eaten from the way you're goin' on about it."

"They've got away with better men than you an' me," Bill answered.

"Oh, hush your croakin'. You make me all-fired tired," said Henry angrily, rolling over on his side. He was surprised that Bill made no similar display of temper. Bill was easily angered by sharp words. Henry thought long over this abnormal behavior before he went to sleep, and as he dozed off, he concluded, "There's no mistakin' it; Bill's almighty blue. I'll have to cheer him up tomorrow."

CHAPTER THREE
THE HUNGER CRY

The day began favorably. They had lost no dogs during the night, and they swung out upon the silent, cold trail with lightened hearts. Bill seemed to have forgotten his concerns of the previous night, and even took it lightly when, at midday, the dogs overturned the sled on a bad piece of trail.

It was an awkward pile-up. The sled was jammed upside down between a tree trunk and a huge rock, and they were forced to unharness the dogs in order to straighten out the tangle. The two men were trying to right the sled when Henry observed One Ear edging away.

"Here, you, One Ear!" he cried, straightening up and turning around on the dog.

But One Ear broke into a run across the snow, his traces trailing behind him. And there, out in the snow of the trail behind them, the she-wolf waited for him. As he neared her, he became suddenly cautious. He slowed down to an alert and mincing walk, and then stopped. He regarded her with caution, but also with desire. She seemed to smile at him, showing her teeth in an inviting, rather than menacing way. She moved toward him a few steps, playfully, and then halted. One Ear drew near to her, still alert and cautious, his tail and ears in the air, his head held high.

He tried to sniff noses with her a few times, but each time she retreated playfully and coyly. Every advance on his part was accompanied by a corresponding retreat on her part. Step by step, she was luring him away from the security of his human companions. Once, as though warned, he turned his head and looked back at the overturned sled, at his teammates, and at the two men who were calling to him. But whatever he was thinking, he forgot when the she-wolf advanced, sniffed noses with him for an instant, and then resumed her coy retreat before his renewed advances.

In the meantime, Bill had thought of the rifle, but it was jammed beneath the overturned sled. By the time Henry had helped him to right the sled, One Ear and the she-wolf were too close together and too far from the men to risk a shot.

Too late, One Ear learned his mistake. First, the two men saw him turn and start to run back toward them. Then they saw a dozen wolves, lean and gray, bounding across the snow to cut off his retreat. Instantly, the she-wolf's coy playfulness disappeared. With a snarl, she sprang upon One Ear. He thrust her off with his shoulder and changed his course in an attempt to circle around to the sled. More wolves were appearing every moment and joining in the chase. The she-wolf was one leap behind One Ear and holding her own.

"Where are you goin'?" Henry suddenly demanded, grabbing his partner's arm.

Bill shook his hand off. "I won't stand it," he said. "They ain't a-goin' to get any more of our dogs if I can help it."

Gun in hand, he plunged into the underbrush beside the trail, moving to cut off the wolves' pursuit. With his rifle, in the broad daylight, it might be possible for him to intimidate the wolves and save the dog.

"Say, Bill!" Henry called after him, as he was lost to view. "Be careful! Don't take no chances!"

Henry sat down on the sled and watched. There was nothing else for him to do. Bill was out of sight, but now and again Henry could see One Ear, appearing and disappearing in the underbrush as the wolves surrounded him. The dog knew he was in danger, but was nearly cut off from the sled by the wolves. It did not appear that One Ear could outrun his pursuers and get back to the sled.

Somewhere out of his sight, Henry knew that the wolf-pack, One Ear, and Bill were coming together. It happened all too quickly. He heard a shot, then two more in rapid succession. Bill's ammunition was gone. Then he heard a great outcry of snarls and yelps. He recognized One Ear's yell of pain and terror, and he heard the cry of a stricken wolf, then nothing more. That was all. The snarls ceased. The yelping died away. Silence settled down again over the lonely land.

He sat for a long while upon the sled. There was no need for him to go and see what had happened. He knew it as though it had taken place before his eyes. Once, he got up and hastily unpacked the axe. But for some time longer, he sat and brooded, the two remaining dogs crouching and trembling at his feet.

At last he arose wearily and proceeded to fasten the dogs to the sled. He passed a rope over his own shoulder and pulled with them, but did not go far. At the first hint of darkness, he camped hurriedly and gathered a generous supply of firewood. He fed the dogs, cooked and ate his supper, and bedded down close to the fire.

But he was not destined to rest. Before his

eyes closed, the wolves were quite visible, dangerously near. They encircled him and the fire, and he could see them plainly in the fire-light, lying down, sitting up, crawling forward on their bellies, or slinking back and forth. They even slept, a luxury he was denied. He kept the fire blazing brightly, the only barrier between his body and their hungry fangs. His two dogs stayed close by, alternately leaning against him and whimpering, and snarling desperately if a wolf came too close. At moments when the dogs snarled, the whole circle would be agitated, the wolves coming to their feet and pressing forward, a chorus of snarls and yelps rising about him. Then the circle would lie down again.

But this circle continued to draw inward. Bit by bit, an inch at a time, with wolves bellying forward here and there, the circle would narrow until the brutes were almost within springing distance. Then, after he hurled flaming branches into the pack, they withdrew hastily, with yelps and frightened snarls when a too-daring animal was scorched.

Morning found the man exhausted, wide-eyed from lack of sleep, but with a task in mind. He cooked breakfast in the darkness. At nine o'clock, with the coming of daylight, the wolf-pack drew back, and he got to work.

Chopping down young saplings, he built a scaffold in the trees. Then, with the aid of the dogs, he hoisted the coffin onto the scaffold.

"They got Bill, an' they may get me, but they'll sure never get you, young man," he said, addressing the dead body in its tree-tomb.

Then he took to the trail with the lightened sled. The dogs were willing; they, too, knew that safety lay in getting to Fort McGurry. The wolves were now more open in their pursuit, trotting quietly behind and ranging along on either side, red tongues lolling, ribs protruding, with strings for muscles. They were so lean that Henry marveled that they did not simply collapse in the snow.

He did not dare continue traveling until dark. At midday, the sun not only warmed the southern horizon, but even thrust its golden upper rim above the skyline. He took it as a sign. The days were growing longer. The sun was returning. He camped just after it departed for the day, and spent the remaining hours of gray daylight and somber twilight chopping an enormous supply of firewood.

With night came horror. Not only were the starving wolves growing bolder, but lack of sleep was wearing Henry down. He dozed despite himself, crouching by the fire, the blankets about his shoulders, the axe between his knees, and on either side a dog pressing close against him. He awoke once and saw a big gray wolf in front of him, one of the largest of the pack, not a dozen feet away. The brute deliberately stretched like a lazy dog, yawning full in his face and looking upon him possessively, as if the man were merely a delayed meal that was soon to be eaten. Perhaps twenty wolves watched him hungrily or slept in the snow, reminding him of children awaiting permission to eat. He wondered how and when the meal would begin.

As he piled wood on the fire, he discovered an appreciation of his own body, which he had never felt before. He watched his moving muscles with fascination, and was interested in the cunning mechanism of his fingers, now and then flexing them. Then he would cast a glance of fear at the wolf-circle drawn expectantly about him. Like a blow, the realization would strike him that this wonderful body of his was simply meat, to be torn and slashed by their hungry fangs, to nourish them as moose and rabbit had often nourished him.

He woke from a doze that was half-nightmare to see the reddish she-wolf before him, watching him wistfully, not more than six feet away. She ignored the two dogs whimpering and snarling at his feet. She was looking at the man, and for some time, he returned her look. There was nothing threatening about her. As he returned her gaze, he knew her to be very hungry. He was the food. Her mouth opened, the saliva drooled forth, and she licked her chops with anticipation.

A spasm of fear went through him. He reached hastily for a flaming branch to throw at her. But before his fingers had closed on it, she sprang back to safety, and he knew that she was used to having things thrown at her. She had snarled as she sprang away, baring her white fangs, in a way that made him shudder. He glanced at his hand, marveling again at its intricate cleverness as it held the fiery wood. In the same instant, he saw a vision of those same sensitive and delicate fingers being crushed and torn by her white teeth. Never had he so valued his own body.

All night he fought off the hungry pack with burning brands. When he dozed despite himself, the whimpering and snarling of the dogs aroused him. Morning came, but for the first time, the light of day failed to scatter the wolves. The man waited in vain for them to go. They remained in a circle about him and his fire, displaying a possessive arrogance that shook his courage that had been restored by the morning light.

He made one desperate attempt to pull out on the trail. But the moment he left the protection of the fire, the boldest wolf leaped for him, but fell short. He saved himself by springing back, the wolf's jaws snapping together a scant six inches from his thigh. The rest of the pack was now up and surging upon him, and it took firebrands thrown right and left to drive them back to a respectful distance.

Even in the daylight he did not dare leave the fire to chop fresh wood. Twenty feet away towered a huge, dead spruce. He spent half the day extending his campfire to the tree, keeping a half dozen burning branches ready to fling. Once at the tree, he studied the surrounding forest in order to fell the tree in the direction of the most firewood.

The night was a repetition of the night before, except that his fatigue was becoming overpowering. The dogs' constant snarling no longer awakened him, even when it changed in volume or pitch. He awoke with a start. The she-wolf was less than a yard away. He thrust a fiery brand right into her open and snarling mouth. She sprang away, yelling with pain, and while he took delight in the smell of burning flesh and hair, he watched her shaking her head and growling angrily twenty feet away.

But this time, before he dozed again, he tied a burning pine-knot to his right hand. His eyes were closed only a few minutes when the burning of the flame on his flesh awakened him. For several hours he followed this routine. Every time he was thus awakened, he drove back the wolves by throwing firebrands, replenished the fire, and rearranged the pine-knot on his hand. This system worked well, but a time came when he did not fasten the pine-knot securely. As his eyes closed, it fell away from his hand.

He dreamed he was in Fort McGurry, warm and comfortable, playing cards with the fort's business agent. It seemed that the fort was besieged by wolves, howling at the very gates. Sometimes he paused from the game to listen and laugh at the futile efforts of the wolves. And then in this strange dream, there was a crash. The door burst open. He could see the wolves flooding into the big living room of the fort. Their howls were much noisier now. They were leaping straight for him and the agent. This howling now bothered him. His dream was merging into something else—he didn't know what, but through it all, following him, persisted the howling.

And then he awoke to find the howling to

be real. There was a great snarling and yelping. The wolves were rushing him. They were
all about him and upon him. The teeth of one
had closed upon his arm. Instinctively, he
leaped into the fire, and as he leaped, he felt
the sharp slash of teeth tear through the flesh
of his leg.

Then a fire fight began. His stout mittens
temporarily protected his hands, and he
scooped live coals into the air in all directions,
until the campfire took on the appearance of
a volcano. But it could not last long. The heat
was blistering his face, singeing his eyebrows
and lashes off, and beginning to burn his feet.
With a flaming brand in each hand, he sprang
to the edge of the fire.

The wolves had been driven back.
Wherever the live coals had fallen, the snow
was sizzling. Now and then a retreating wolf
stepped on one and leaped with a wild snarl of
pain. Flinging firebrands at the nearest of his
enemies, the man thrust his smoldering mittens into the snow and stamped about to cool
his feet.

His two dogs were missing, and he knew
well that they had become courses in the
extended meal which had begun days before
with Fatty. In the days to follow, he would
likely be the meal's last course.

"You ain't got me yet!" he cried, savagely shaking his fist at the hungry beasts. At the sound of his voice, the whole circle was agitated. There was a general snarl, and the she-wolf slid up close to him across the snow and watched him with wistful hunger.

He set to work to carry out a new idea that had come to him. He extended the fire into a large circle and crouched inside it, his sleeping outfit under him as a protection against the melting snow. When he had disappeared within his shelter of flame, the whole pack came curiously to the rim of the fire to see what had become of him. Until now, they had been denied access to the fire's warmth, and they settled down in a close-drawn circle, like so many dogs, blinking and yawning and stretching their lean bodies in the unaccustomed heat. Then the she-wolf sat down, pointed her nose at a star, and began to howl. One by one, the wolves joined her, till the whole pack, with noses pointed skyward, was howling its hungry cry.

Dawn came, and daylight. The fire was burning low, and the fuel had run out. The man attempted to step out of his circle of flame to get more, but the wolves surged to meet him. Burning branches made them spring aside, but they no longer sprang back.

In vain, he strove to drive them back. As he gave up and stumbled back inside his circle, a wolf leaped for him, missed, and landed with all four feet in the coals. It cried out with terror, snarled, and scrambled back to cool its paws in the snow.

The man crouched down on his blankets, leaning forward from the hips. His shoulders relaxed and drooping, and his head on his knees, advertised that he had given up the struggle. Now and again he raised his head to note the dying down of the fire. The circle of flame and coals was breaking into segments with openings in between. The openings grew in size; the segments of fire diminished.

"I guess you can come an' get me any time," he mumbled. "Anyway, I'm goin' to sleep."

Once he awakened, and in an opening in the circle, directly in front of him, he saw the she-wolf gazing at him.

Again he awakened, a little later, though it seemed hours to him. A mysterious change had taken place, so mysterious that he was shocked wider awake. Something had happened. He could not understand at first. Then he discovered it. The wolves were gone. Only the trampled snow remained to show how closely they had pressed in on him. Sleep was overtaking him again, his head sinking down upon his knees, when he roused with a sudden start.

There were cries of men, the churn of sleds, the creaking of harnesses, and the eager whimpering of straining dogs. Four sleds pulled in from the riverbed to the camp among the trees. Half a dozen men were gathered about the man who crouched in the center of the dying fire. They were shaking and prodding him into consciousness. He looked at them like a drunken man and mumbled sleepily.

"Red she-wolf. . . . Come in with the dogs at feedin' time. . . . First she ate the dog-food. . . . Then she ate the dogs. . . . An' after that she ate Bill. . . ."

"Where's Lord Alfred?" one of the men bellowed in his ear, shaking him roughly.

He shook his head slowly. "No, she didn't eat him. . . . He's roostin' in a tree at the last camp."

"Dead?" the man shouted.

"An' in a box," Henry answered. He jerked his shoulder away from the grip of his questioner. "Say, you lemme alone. . . . I'm jes' plumb tuckered out. . . . Goo' night, everybody."

His eyes fluttered and shut. His chin fell

forward on his chest. And even as they eased him down upon the blankets, his snores were rising on the frosty air.

But there was another sound. Far and faint it was, in the remote distance, the cry of the hungry wolf-pack as it took to the trail of other meat than the man it had just missed.

PART TWO:
BORN OF THE WILD

CHAPTER ONE
THE BATTLE OF THE FANGS

It was the she-wolf who had first heard the voices of men and the whining of the sled-dogs, and it was she who was first to give up on the cornered man in his circle of dying flames. The other wolves had been unwilling to give up on the kill they had hunted down, but after hanging back for a few minutes, they followed on the trail made by the she-wolf.

A large gray wolf led the pack. He steered them on the heels of the she-wolf, snarling and snapping at any younger member who dared try to pass him. When he saw the she-wolf trotting slowly across the snow, he increased the pace.

She dropped into the leadership position to his right. He did not threaten her when she passed him. On the contrary, he seemed kindly disposed toward her. When he ran too close, she was the one who snarled and showed her teeth. But he showed no anger. He just sprang aside and ran clumsily ahead.

She had more troubles than he did. On her right side, as always, ran a gaunt, scarred, one-eyed old wolf. He, too, would crowd her. As she did with the large gray wolf on her left, she corrected this habit with her teeth. However, whenever both males tried to get near her at the same time, she had to snap at both of them, while continuing to lead the hungry pack.

Each time the old wolf dodged away from the she-wolf's sharp teeth, he ran into a young, full-grown, spirited three-year-old male who ran even with him on his blind right side. When the young wolf edged ahead of his elder, he was punished with a snarl and a snap. Sometimes he dared hang back and try to edge in between the older wolf and the she-wolf. Then all three of them would turn on him, and he would halt suddenly in a defensive stance. This in turn caused the short-tempered, hungry wolves behind him to bang into him, earning him sharp, angry nips from them. He kept it up anyway, gaining nothing but pain and future trouble.

Had it not been for hunger, there would have been fights over the she-wolf and the pack leadership, which would have broken up the pack. But the situation of the pack was too desperate for that. They were lean and slow from starvation. At the front were the strongest; at the rear were the very young and the very old. Yet all were more like skeletons than full-bodied wolves. Nevertheless, the movements of the animals were effortless and tireless.

They ran many miles that day. They ran through the night and into the next day over the surface of a world frozen and dead. No life stirred. They alone were alive, and they sought other things that were alive so they might devour them and continue to live.

They crossed a number of small valleys and streams before coming upon a big bull moose, unguarded by mysterious fires or flaming missiles. They were familiar with the hooves and antlers of moose, and abandoned their usual caution for a brief, fierce fight. The big-antlered bull tore open the wolves, split their skulls, and trampled them into the snow. But he was doomed. He went down, with the she-wolf tearing savagely at his throat, and with other teeth devouring him even before he ceased to struggle. He weighed over eight hundred pounds—twenty pounds of meat for each of the forty-odd wolves, but they were as good at eating as they were at fasting. Within hours, only a few scattered bones remained of the once-impressive moose.

The pack now rested and slept. With full stomachs, the younger males began to bicker, and this continued for a few days before the pack broke up. The famine was over. The wolves were now in a land with plenty of game. They still hunted as a pack, but were now more cautious, separating heavy cows or crippled old bulls from the small moose-herds they ran across.

There came a day, in this land of plenty, when the wolf-pack split in two. The she-wolf, the young leader on her left, and the one-eyed elder on her right, led their half of the pack down to the Mackenzie River and across into the lake country. Each day the pack got smaller. Two by two, male and female, the wolves were deserting. Occasionally a lone male was driven out by the sharp teeth of his rivals. In the end there remained only four: the she-wolf, the young leader, the old one-eyed wolf, and the ambitious three-year-old.

By now the she-wolf had developed a ferocious temper. Her three suitors all bore her teeth-marks, but they never fought back. Instead, they tried to placate her. Toward one another, though, they were very fierce. The three-year-old, young and strong, finally grew too ambitious. He caught the one-eyed elder on his blind side and shredded his ear. But the grizzled old fellow's missing eye and scarred muzzle showed his long years of experience. He knew exactly what to do.

The battle began fairly, but it didn't end that way. The third wolf joined the elder and, together, both leaders attacked and destroyed the ambitious three-year-old with their merciless fangs. Forgotten were their hunts together, the shared game, their shared famine. The business of love was at hand, crueler than that of finding food. Meanwhile, the she-wolf sat down contentedly on her haunches and watched them fight over her. She was even pleased. This was her day.

And in this business of love, the three-year-old gave up his life. On either side of the body stood his two rivals, gazing at the she-wolf, who sat smiling in the snow. But the elder leader was as wise in love as in battle. The younger leader turned his head to lick a wound on his shoulder, exposing his neck to his rival, who saw his chance out of his single eye. He darted in low, bit with a long, ripping slash that reached the great vein of the other male's throat, then leaped clear.

The young leader snarled terribly, but the

snarl gave way to a tickling cough. Bleeding, he sprang at the elder and fought until his legs weakened and the light of life faded from his eyes. His springs fell shorter and shorter. All the while, the she-wolf. the cause of it all, just sat back and smiled, pleased by the battle.

When the young leader lay dead in the snow, One Eye stalked over to the she-wolf with mingled triumph and caution, expecting to be snapped at in the usual way. He was surprised when she did not bare her teeth in anger. She sniffed noses with him, and even leaped about and played with him like a puppy. And he, for all his gray years and experience, behaved quite as puppyishly and even a little more foolishly. The beaten rivals and the battles were forgotten, except for once when old One Eye stopped for a moment to lick his wounds. Then, involuntarily, his lips started to snarl, and the hair of his neck and shoulders bristled, while he prepared to spring. But it was all forgotten at the next moment, when he sprang after the she-wolf, who led him on a chase through the woods.

After that, they ran side by side, like good friends who have reached an understanding. The days passed. They hunted and ate together. After a time, the she-wolf began to grow restless. She seemed to be searching for something she could not find. She spent a lot of time nosing about under fallen trees, rocks, and overhanging banks. Old One Eye was not interested at all, but he followed her good-naturedly. When she took a long time to investigate a particular place, he would lie down and wait until she was ready to go on.

They kept traveling back toward the Mackenzie River, following it slowly downriver. They made hunting trips up along the small streams that entered it, and then returned. Sometimes they met other wolves, usually in pairs, but there was no friendliness displayed on either side, no desire to form a pack. Several times they met solitary wolves, always males, who insisted on trying to join with One Eye and his mate. He resented them, and when she stood shoulder to shoulder with him, bristling and showing her teeth, the hopeful lone wolves would back off and continue on their lonely way.

One moonlit night, running through the quiet forest, One Eye suddenly halted. His muzzle went up, his tail stiffened, and his nostrils widened. He held up one foot as he sniffed the air and tried to figure out what his nose was telling him. One casual sniff had satisfied his mate, and she trotted on to reassure him. He followed her, still suspicious, halting now and then to study the warning carefully.

The she-wolf crept out cautiously onto the edge of a large, open space amidst the trees. For some time she stood alone. Then One Eye, creeping and crawling,every sense on careful alert, joined her. They stood side by side, watching and listening and smelling.

They heard dogs scuffling, men's low-pitched cries, the sharper voices of scolding women, and once the shrill cry of a child. They could see little except the huge bulks of animal-hide lodges, people moving past the fire, and the slowly rising smoke. But they could smell the many smells of an Indian camp. These meant nothing to One Eye, but the she-wolf knew every detail.

She was strangely stirred, and sniffed and sniffed with increasing delight. But One Eye was doubtful, and nervously started to go. She turned and nuzzled him in a reassuring way, then looked at the camp again with a new wistfulness. She felt a thrilling desire that urged her to go forward. She wanted to be closer to that fire, to squabble with the dogs, and to be dodging the men's stumbling feet.

One Eye moved impatiently beside her. She grew restless, feeling again the pressing need to find the thing for which she searched. She turned and trotted back into the forest, to the great relief of One Eye, who trotted in front until they were well within the shelter of the trees.

As they slid silently along in the moonlight, they spotted tracks. Both noses went down to the fresh footprints in the snow. One Eye ran ahead cautiously, his mate at his heels. Then One Eye caught sight of a dim, white movement in the snow. He broke into a full run in pursuit of the bounding white patch, racing with his mate along a narrow alley flanked by spruce. He was rapidly overtaking the speedy white shape. Bound by bound he gained. Finally, when he was one leap from sinking his teeth into it, the white shape now became a struggling snowshoe rabbit. It jumped high in the air above him, dancing in mid-air without falling.

One Eye sprang back in sudden fright, then crouched and snarled at the rabbit, whose movement seemed so odd. The she-wolf coolly thrust past him. She paused for a moment, then sprang for the dancing rabbit, leaping but missing as her teeth clipped emptily together with a metallic snap. She made another leap, then another. Displeased with her repeated failures, her mate tried again, leaping and briefly catching the rabbit. But the downward movement of a spruce sapling frightened him into letting go, leaving the rabbit dancing in the air again. He leaped backward, snarling in rage and fright.

The she-wolf angrily sank her fangs into her mate's shoulder, and in his frightened confusion, he struck back for once, ripping down the side of her muzzle. Now she was even angrier, for she did not expect him to fight back when punished, and sprang upon him with even more fury. Realizing his mistake, he tried to pacify her, but she penalized him with her teeth until he gave up the effort and simply turned his head away.

In the meantime, the rabbit danced above them in the air. The she-wolf sat down in the snow, and old One Eye, now more afraid of her than of the strange sapling, sprang and caught the rabbit again, watching the sapling as it again bent to the earth with him. This time, he kept hold of the game and remained still, tasting and enjoying its blood. Finally his mate came over, took the rabbit from him, and gnawed its head off. The sapling shot up into its normal position, giving them no more grief, and they began to devour the rabbit.

There were other trails where rabbits were hanging in the air, and the wolf-pair hunted them all, the she-wolf leading the way, old One Eye following and observant, learning how to rob bent-tree snares—knowledge sure to be useful in the days to come.

CHAPTER TWO
THE LAIR

For two days, the she-wolf and One Eye hung about the Indian camp. He was worried, yet his mate hesitated to leave. But after a rifle bullet from the camp smashed against a tree trunk near One Eye's head, they quickly put several miles between themselves and the danger.

They traveled for only a couple of days. The she-wolf's search was now desperate; she was getting very heavy and slow. Once, chasing a rabbit that she would normally have caught with ease, she had to lie down to rest. One Eye came to nuzzle her. But when he touched her, she snapped so fiercely at him that he tumbled over backward, looking ridiculous. Her temper was now shorter than ever, but he had become more patient than ever.

And then she found it. It was up a small stream that flowed to the MacKenzie River in summer and froze solid in winter. The she-wolf was trotting wearily along, her mate well ahead, when she came upon the high, overhanging clay-bank. She turned aside and trotted over.

The wear and tear of nature had worn away the riverbank, creating a small cave. She paused at the opening to inspect it with great care. It was a dry, cozy, round chamber, six feet wide, with a narrow mouth. One Eye had returned and watched her patiently. Finally, with a tired sigh, she entered the cave. One Eye laughed at her with ears pointed in interest, and she could see the brush of his tail waving good-naturedly. Her own ears lay back and down for a moment, and her tongue hung peaceably out, showing her satisfaction.

One Eye was hungry. Though he lay down in the entrance and slept, his sleep was fitful. He kept waking up and cocking his ears at the bright April sun. When he dozed, he heard the faint whispers of hidden trickles of running water, and would rouse himself and listen intently. The sun had come back. Life was stirring. The feel of spring was in the air, under the snow, and in the trees.

He glanced anxiously at his mate, but she showed no desire to get up. He looked outside and saw half a dozen snow-birds, but dozed off again when the she-wolf stayed put. A tiny, shrill noise nagged at him. He sleepily brushed his nose with his paw a couple of times, and then awoke. There, buzzing in the air at the tip of his nose, was a big mosquito, one that had lain frozen in a dry log all winter and was now thawed. He could resist the call of the world no longer, and he was hungry.

He crawled over to his mate and tried get her moving, but she only snarled at him. Alone, he exited into the bright sunshine, and found the going difficult in the soft snow. He headed up the frozen bed of the stream, where the snow, shaded by the trees was still hard enough to walk on. He was gone eight hours, and came back through the darkness, even hungrier than when he started. He had broken through the melting snow crust and wallowed, while the snowshoe rabbits had skimmed along on top, lightly as ever.

He paused with sudden suspicion at the mouth of the cave. Faint, strange sounds came from within, not made by his mate, but somehow familiar. He crept cautiously inside and was met by a warning snarl from the she-wolf, which he received and obeyed calmly. But the other sounds, faint and slobbery, continued to interest him.

Irritated, his mate warned him away, so he curled up and slept in the entrance. When morning came, he again investigated the remotely familiar sounds. There was a new, jealous note in his mate's warning snarl, one that he heeded. But sheltering against the length of her body, he was surprised to see five blind, helpless little bundles of life, making tiny whimpering noises. Though he had seen this many times in his long life, the surprise remained fresh each time.

His mate looked at him anxiously, growling and snarling at him every once in a while. Although she had never actually seen it happen, in her instinct there lurked an ancestral memory of fathers who had eaten their helpless newborn cubs. This memory told her to warn One Eye away from a close inspection of their children. But there was no danger. Old One Eye was feeling an ancient urge of his own, one he did not question. It was the most natural thing in the world that he should leave his newborn family to go hunt up some meat, so he left the shelter and headed up the frozen stream.

Five or six miles from the lair, the stream forked. On the way up the left fork, he came upon a fresh track. He smelled it and found it so fresh that he crouched swiftly to see where it went. The footprint was much larger than his own, and he knew that this type of trail offered him little meat. He turned back deliberately and took the right fork.

Half a mile up the right fork, his quick ears caught a gnawing sound. It was a porcupine, chewing on the bark of a tree. One Eye approached carefully, but without hope. Although he knew porcupines, never in his whole life had he eaten one. But he had long since learned that there was such a thing as luck, so he continued to draw near. Something new might happen.

The porcupine rolled itself into a ball, with long, sharp needles in all directions. In his youth, One Eye had once sniffed too near a similar, apparently inert ball of quills, and had the tail flick out suddenly in his face. One quill had stayed in his muzzle for weeks, a constant burning pain, until it finally worked its way out. So he crouched comfortably, his nose out of tail-swat range, to wait in silence. There was no telling what might occur. The porcupine might unroll and expose its unguarded belly to a ripping paw. After half an hour, he arose, growled angrily at the ball, and left. He had waited in this way too often before, without any reward, so he decided not to waste any more time. As the day wore on, he found no more game.

His deep, strong instinct of fatherhood told him that he must find meat. In the afternoon he came out of a thicket and stumbled upon a grouse. The slow-witted bird was sitting on a log a foot away, and began to rise in fright. But One Eye smashed it to earth with a paw and caught it in his mouth. As his teeth crunched through the tender flesh and fragile bones, he began to eat. Then he remembered, and started for home with the grouse in his mouth.

A mile above the forks, running with quiet caution, he came upon more recent imprints of the large tracks he had discovered in the early morning. He followed the tracks, prepared to meet their maker at every turn of the stream.

At a large bend in the stream, he slid his head around a corner of rock and saw something that sent him crouching swiftly down. It was the maker of the tracks, a large female lynx. She was crouching just as he had done once that day, near the tight-rolled ball of quills. He became even more silent and shadowy than before, as he crept and circled around to get downwind of the silent, motionless pair.

He lay down in the snow, dropped the grouse, and watched the lynx and the porcupine. Each was intent on life, but their goals in life were opposite. One Eye crouched in hiding, hoping for a strange event that might help him on the meat-trail that was his own goal in life.

Half an hour passed, and then an hour. Nothing happened. The ball of quills might have been a stone, the lynx might have been marble, and old One Eye might have been dead. Yet all three animals were tensely alive, alert in their absolute stillness.

One Eye moved slightly and peered out with increased eagerness. Something was happening. The porcupine had finally decided that its enemy had gone away. Slowly, cautiously, it was unrolling from its armored ball. One Eye felt a sudden, involuntary watering in his mouth, excited by the living meat that was opening up before him.

The porcupine had nearly unrolled when the lynx struck like a flash, its claws ripping the tender belly open. If the porcupine had been entirely unrolled, or if it had not discovered its enemy a bit sooner, the paw would have escaped unhurt. But a side-flick of the tail sank sharp quills into the paw as it came away. The the big cat screamed in sudden pain and surprise. One Eye half arose in his excitement, his ears up, his tail straight out and quivering.

The lynx lost her temper and sprang savagely at the thing that had hurt her. But the porcupine, squealing and grunting and trying to roll back up into its protective ball, flicked out its tail again, and again the big cat screamed with pain. Then she backed away and began sneezing, her nose bristling with quills. Trying to dislodge the fiery darts, she brushed her nose with her paws, thrust it into the snow, and rubbed it against twigs and branches, all the while leaping about in a frenzy of pain and fright, until she finally quieted down for a minute.

One Eye watched. Even he could not suppress a start and an involuntary bristling of hair along his back when the lynx suddenly leaped straight up in the air, emitted a terrible cry, and sprang away up the trail, screaming with every leap.

Only when her racket had died out in the distance, did One Eye venture forth. He walked as delicately as if the snow were carpeted with porcupine quills. The porcupine met One Eye's approach with a furious squealing and a clashing of its long teeth. It had managed to roll up in a ball again, but it was not quite the old compact ball. It could no longer do that; it had been ripped almost in half and was bleeding badly.

One Eye scooped out mouthfuls of the blood-soaked snow, and chewed and tasted and swallowed. This increased his hunger mightily, but he was too wise to forget his caution. He lay down and waited, while the dying porcupine ground its teeth, squealed, and sobbed. In a little while, One Eye noticed that the quills were drooping. The porcupine quivered greatly for a moment, then gave one final, defiant clash of the long teeth. All the quills drooped, and the body relaxed and moved no more.

With a nervous paw, One Eye stretched out the porcupine and turned it over. Nothing happened; it was surely dead. He studied it intently for a moment, then picked it up with care and started off down the stream, partly carrying and partly dragging the porcupine alongside him to avoid stepping on the quills. Then he remembered something, dropped the burden, and trotted back to where he had left the grouse. He knew that he should now eat the bird, did so, then returned and took up the porcupine again.

When he dragged the result of his day's hunt into the cave, the she-wolf inspected it, turned her muzzle to him, and lightly licked him on the neck. But the next instant she was warning him away from the cubs with a snarl that was less harsh than usual, and more apologetic than menacing. Her instinctive fear of the father of her babies was decreasing. He was behaving as a wolf-father should, showing no unholy desire to devour the young lives that she had brought into the world.

CHAPTER THREE
THE GRAY CUB

He was different from his brothers and sisters. Their fur already showed their mother's reddish coloring, while he was the one little gray cub of the litter. He had inherited old One Eye's pure wolf blood, and was in fact just like him, except that he had both eyes.

The gray cub's eyes had not been open long, yet already he could see clearly. Even while his eyes were still closed, he had felt, tasted, and smelled. He knew his two brothers and his two sisters very well. He had begun to play with them in a feeble, awkward way. He even squabbled with them, his little throat making a strange, rasping noise that would one day be a growl.

And while still blind, he had learned by other senses to know his mother, who was a source of warmth and liquid food and tenderness. She possessed a gentle tongue that soothed his soft little body with gentle caresses, lulling him to sleep. He had slept for most of his first month of life, but now he stayed awake longer. The world he knew was dimly lit and small, but knowing no other, its smallness never bothered him.

But one wall of his world was different—

the mouth of the cave, the source of light. It had attracted him before his eyes opened, as its light had sent warm, pleasing little flashes through his sealed eyelids. He was drawn toward it as a plant is drawn toward the sun. Even from the beginning, he and his brothers and sisters had crawled toward the mouth of the cave, instinctively drawn more and more to its light.

In this way, the gray cub learned another side of his mother. At first she nudged him sharply away from the opening, then later batted him away from it with a correcting paw, which hurt. He learned to avoid pain by not risking it—or when he did, by dodging and retreating. His first notions about the world were about how to avoid hurt.

He and his brothers and sisters were fierce little cubs, as was to be expected of a breed of meat-killers and meat-eaters. His father and mother ate only meat. His first milk had been transformed directly from meat. Now, at a month old, when his eyes had been open for but a week, he, too, was beginning to eat meat that the she-wolf had already half-digested and brought back up, since she no longer had enough milk to feed her cubs completely.

He was also the fiercest of the litter, with

tiny rages much more terrible than those of the others. He could make a louder rasping growl than any of them. He was the first to learn the trick of rolling a fellow-cub over with a cunning paw-stroke, or gripping another cub by the ear, and then pulling and tugging and growling through tightly clenched jaws. Of the five, he was the hardest for his mother to keep inside the cave.

The light fascinated the gray cub more each day. He was always leaving on small adventures that took him toward the cave's entrance, and he was always driven back. He did not know it as an entrance, only as a wall of light. It was the sun of his world, attracting him as a candle attracts a moth. His swiftly expanding life urged him constantly toward it, his destiny, though he knew nothing of the outside at all.

There was one strange thing about this wall of light. He knew his father as the one other dweller in the world, one similar to his mother, who slept near the light and brought meat. But he did not understand how his father could walk right into the far, white wall and disappear. The gray cub had approached the other walls, bumped his tender nose, felt hurt, and then left them alone. He accepted this vanishing into the wall as a thing of his father, as milk and half-digested meat were things of his mother.

The gray cub did not think as men did, but his conclusions were as clear as theirs. He didn't care why a thing happened, just how it happened. Thus, after bumping his nose on the other walls a few times, he simply accepted that he could not disappear into walls as his father did. He was not curious about the reason for this difference. It just was.

Like most creatures of the Wild, he knew starvation early in life. There came a time when there was no longer any meat or even milk. At first, the cubs whimpered and cried, but for the most part they slept. Soon they were reduced to a coma of hunger. There were no more squabbles or growls or tiny rages. The adventures toward the far white wall ceased. The cubs slept, while the life inside them flickered and died down.

One Eye was desperate. He ranged far and wide, and slept very little in the now-cheerless lair. The she-wolf even left her litter in search of meat. In the first days after the cubs' birth, One Eye had gone back to the Indian camp several times, and robbed the rabbit snares. But now, with the melting of the ice and snow, the Indian camp had moved away, and that source of meat was gone.

When the gray cub awoke and again took interest in the far, white wall, only one sister was left. As he grew stronger, he had to play alone, for the sister no longer moved about. His little body rounded out with the meat he now ate, but the food had come too late for her. Reduced to a skeleton wrapped in skin, she slept until the flame of her life flickered and died out.

At the end of a second and less severe famine, the time came when the gray cub no longer saw his father. The she-wolf knew why One Eye never came back, but there was no way for her to explain this to the gray cub. She had gone hunting for meat up the left fork of the stream where the lynx lived, and had found his remains at the end of the trail. There were many signs of battle, and of the lynx's return to her lair after having won the fight. Although the she-wolf had found the lynx's lair, the signs told her that the big cat was inside, and so she had not dared to go in.

After that, the she-wolf avoided the left fork when hunting, for she knew that the lynx's lair contained a litter of kittens. She also knew the lynx to be a fierce, bad-tempered creature and a terrifying fighter. It was one thing for half a dozen wolves to drive a single spitting, bristling lynx up a tree. It was quite a different matter for a lone wolf to meet a lynx—especially one known to have a litter of hungry kittens.

But the Wild is the Wild. And motherhood is motherhood—fiercely protective in or out of the Wild. The time would come when the she-wolf, for her gray cub's sake, would have to brave the left fork, and the lair in the rocks, and the fury of the lynx.

CHAPTER FOUR
THE WALL OF THE WORLD

By the time his mother began leaving the cave on hunting trips, the cub had learned that his mother's law ordered him not to approach the entrance. The law had been enforced with her nose and paws. However, he was also developing the instinct of fear. Having lived his whole young life in the cave, he had never met anything to be afraid of, but fear was a deep instinct in him, handed down through One Eye and the she-wolf by every generation of wolves that had gone before, and common to every animal. Fear—the legacy of the Wild which no animal may escape.

So without fully understanding why, the gray cub knew fear. He accepted it as as one of life's restrictions. He also knew other restrictions: the inability to satisfy hunger, the hardness of the cave-wall, the sharp nudge of his mother's nose and the smashing stroke of her paw. He had learned that there was not always freedom, that there were laws. If he obeyed them, he could escape hurt and be happy, so he simply classified the things that hurt and the things that didn't.

Thus, obedient to his mother's law and to his sense of fear, he kept away from the mouth of the cave. It remained a white wall of light. When his mother was absent, he slept most of the time; when awake, he kept very quiet. Once, lying awake, he heard a strange sound in the white wall. He did not know that it was a wolverine, scenting out the cave. The cub knew only that the sniff was something strange, and therefore terrifying, for the unknown was one of the chief elements of fear.

The hair on the gray cub's back bristled silently. How could he know that he should bristle at this thing which sniffed? It was the visible expression of the fear inside him, something he could not explain. With fear came another instinct—concealment. The cub was in a frenzy of terror, yet he lay without movement or sound, to all appearances dead. His mother, coming home, growled as she smelled the wolverine's track, and bounded into the cave and licked and nuzzled him with unusual affection. The cub felt that somehow he had escaped a great hurt.

But there were other forces at work in the cub, the greatest of which was growth. Instinct and law demanded that he obey, but growth required that he disobey. His growth instinct pushed him ever toward the white wall of light, against his mother's law and his own fear. With every breath he took, and every mouthful of meat he swallowed, the tide of life was rising within him, drawing him to the light. One day, life overcame fear and obedience, and the cub sprawled toward the entrance.

Unlike any other wall he'd known, this wall seemed to vanish as he approached. His tender, hesitant little nose hit no hard surface. He entered what had been the wall and bathed in the light. It was bewildering, and the light grew brighter. Fear urged him to go back, but growth drove him on. Suddenly he found himself at the mouth of the cave.

The light had become painfully bright. He was dazzled by it. He was made dizzy by this abrupt expansion of space. But as his eyes adjusted to the brightness and distance of objects, the wall became more remote and varied. It had changed into the trees along the stream, the mountain above them, and the sky above that.

A great fear came upon him. This was more of the terrible unknown. He crouched down on the lip of the cave and gazed out on the world. He was very much afraid. Because it was unknown, it was hostile to him. The hair stood up on end along his back, and his lips wrinkled weakly in an attempt at a ferocious snarl. Puny and afraid, he challenged and menaced the whole wide world.

Nothing happened. He continued to gaze, and became so interested that he forgot to snarl. He also forgot to be afraid. For the time, fear was replaced by growth, now in the form of curiosity. He began to notice near objects: an open portion of the stream that flashed in the sun, the blasted pine tree that stood at the base of the slope, and the slope itself—beginning just past the lip of the cave and leading down from it.

Until now, the gray cub had lived all his days on a level floor. He had never experienced the hurt of a fall. He did not know what a fall was. So he stepped boldly out upon the air. His hind legs still rested on the cave-lip, so he fell down headfirst. The earth struck him a harsh blow on the nose, making him yelp. Then he began tumbling down the slope.

He was in a panic of terror. The unknown had caught him at last and was about to hurt him badly. Fear had again won out over growth, and he cried out with a sort of *ki-yi*, like a frightened puppy. This was not just fear, but terror. It was different from crouching in frozen fear while the unknown lurked outside. The unknown had caught him, and silence was useless. Down he rolled.

But the slope grew more gradual, and its base was grass-covered, slowing his tumble. When at last he slowed to a stop, he gave one last, agonized yelp and then a long, whimpering wail. Then, as though he had done this a thousand times before, he proceeded to lick away the dry clay that covered him.

After that, he sat up and gazed about this completely unknown world. The cub had broken through the wall of the world. The unknown had let go of its hold on him, and he was unhurt. He was an explorer in a totally new world, filled with curiosity. He now forgot that the unknown held terrors. He was aware only of the curiosity in all the things about him. He inspected the grass beneath him, the mossberry plant just beyond, and the dead trunk of the blasted pine that stood on the edge of a clearing. A squirrel ran around the base of the trunk and gave him a great fright. He cowered down and snarled. But the squirrel was just as scared. It ran up the tree, and from a point of safety chattered back savagely.

This helped the cub's courage, and though the woodpecker he encountered next startled him, he proceeded confidently on his way. He was so confident that when a moosebird carelessly hopped up to him, he reached out at it with a playful paw. The result was a sharp peck on his nose, which made him cower down and *ki-yi*. The noise he made scared the bird away.

But the cub was learning. His misty little mind had figured out that there were live things and things not alive, and that he must watch out for the live things. The things not alive always remained in one place, but the live things moved about, and there was no telling what they might do. The thing to expect of them was the unexpected, and for this he must be prepared.

He traveled very clumsily, misjudging distances and running into things. The surface was uneven. Sometimes he overstepped and stubbed his nose, or understepped and stubbed his feet.

His new world lacked the stability of the cave. Pebbles and stones turned under him when he stepped on them, teaching him that small things that were not alive were more likely to fall down or turn over than large things. But with every mistake he was learning to walk better, to adjust, to measure distances, and to know his own limits.

He had some beginner's luck. Though he did not know it, he was born to hunt meat, and he stumbled upon it just outside his own cave-door. He had tried to walk along the trunk of a fallen pine, but the rotten bark caved in under him. With a despairing yelp, he fell off the trunk and tumbled right into a cleverly hidden bird's nest, landing right in the middle of seven grouse chicks.

They made noises, scaring him at first. Then he realized that they were very little, and he became bolder. They moved. He placed his paw on one, and it moved faster. He enjoyed this. Next he smelled the chick, and then picked it up in his mouth. It struggled and tickled his tongue. At the same time he became aware of a sensation of hunger. His jaws closed together. Fragile bones crunched, and warm blood ran in his mouth, tasting good. This was meat, the same as his mother gave him. But this meat was alive between his teeth and, therefore, better. So he ate that grouse, and then another, and finally all seven chicks. Then, just like his mother, he licked his chops and began to crawl out of the bush.

A feathered whirlwind hit him. He was confused and blinded by the rush of it and the beat of angry wings. He hid his head between his paws and yelped. The blows of the furious mother grouse increased. Then he became angry and rose up, snarling, striking out with his paws. He sank his tiny teeth into one of the wings, and pulled and tugged sturdily. The grouse struggled against him and cried out, pounding him with her free wing. Against her will, he dragged her into the open.

It was his first battle. He was elated. He forgot all about the unknown. He was no longer afraid of anything. He was fighting, tearing at a live thing that was striking at him. And this live thing was meat. He had just destroyed little live things. He would now destroy a big live thing. It was his first taste of the lust to kill, his first awareness of the fighting heritage that destined him to battle for meat. He was thrilled and exulted in ways new to him and greater than any he had known before.

After a time, the grouse became still. The cub still held her by the wing, and they lay on the ground and looked at each other. He tried to growl threateningly, ferociously. She began pecking at him over and over again on his hurting nose. He winced and then whimpered, but still held on as she kept pecking. After a time he tried to back away, not realizing that as long as he continued to hold on to her, the pecking of his abused nose also continued. The fury of fight faded in him. Releasing his prey, he turned and scampered across the open in retreat.

He lay down to rest on the other side of the open space, his tongue lolling out, his chest heaving and panting, still whimpering at the hurt in his nose. Suddenly there came to him a feeling of something unknown and terrible about to happen. Instinctively, he shrank back into the shelter of the bush. As he did so, he felt a breeze, and a large hawk barely missed him as it swept silently past.

While he lay in the bush recovering from his fright, the mother-grouse fluttered out of the raided nest. Distracted by her loss, she did not notice the danger from the sky. But the cub saw, and it was a warning and a lesson to him—the swift downward swoop of the hawk, the skim of its body just above the ground, the strike of its talons in the body of the grouse, the grouse's squawk of agony and fright, and the hawk's rush upward into the blue, carrying the grouse away.

It was a long time before the cub left his shelter. He had learned much. Live things were meat, and good to eat. When they were large enough, they could give hurt. It was better to eat small live things, like grouse chicks, and to let alone large live things, like grouse hens. However, he also felt ambition, a sneaking desire to have another battle with the hen, but the hawk had carried her away. He would go and see if there were other grouse hens.

He came down a bank to the stream, which at this spot widened to a smooth pool twenty feet across. He had never seen water before. It had a smooth surface, and it looked as if he could walk on it. He stepped boldly out onto it and sank, crying with fear, into the unknown. It was cold and he gasped, breathing quickly. The water rushed into his lungs, which had before always breathed in air. The suffocation he experienced felt like death. He hadn't experienced death, but like every animal of the Wild, he instinctively feared death as the greatest of hurts, the sum of the terrors of the unknown.

He surfaced, inhaled sweet air, and instinctively began to swim. The near bank was only a few feet away, but he had come up with his back to it, and the first thing he saw was the opposite bank. So he swam toward it right away. Halfway across, the current grabbed the cub and pulled him downstream into rapidly swirling waters. Now he could not swim at all. The quiet water had suddenly become angry. He bobbed up and down, and was tossed about and smashed against rocks, yelping as he hit each one.

The rapids gave way to a second pool, and

here a small crosscurrent pulled him ashore, washing him gently up onto a bed of gravel. He crawled frantically out of the water and lay down. He had learned something new— water. Water was not alive, yet it moved. It looked as solid as the earth, but was not solid at all. His conclusion was that things were not always as they seemed. The cub's natural fear of the unknown was now strengthened by experience. From now on, he would not trust appearances. He would have to learn what a thing really was before he could trust it.

One other adventure lay ahead of him that day. Remembering his mother, he now wanted her more than anything else in the world. His little body was worn out from adventures. His brain was also tired, for it had never before worked so hard. He was also sleepy. Feeling very lonely and helpless, he started out to look for the cave and his mother.

He was sprawling along between some bushes, when he heard a sharp, threatening cry. There was a flash of yellow before his eyes. It was a weasel, leaping swiftly away from him. This was a small live thing that he did not fear. Then, at his feet, he saw an extremely small live thing that was only several inches long. It was a young weasel, young like himself. It, too, had disobeyed and gone out adventuring. It tried to retreat from him. He turned it over with his paw, and it made an odd, grating noise. The next moment, the flash of yellow reappeared with another menacing cry, and the mother-weasel's sharp teeth bit into the side of his neck.

While he yelped and *ki-yi*'d and scrambled backward, he saw the mother-weasel grab her baby and disappear with it into the woods. The bite-wound in his neck still hurt, but his feelings were even more hurt. So he sat down and whimpered weakly. This mother-weasel was so small and so savage. He had yet to discover that, pound for pound, the weasel was the most ferocious and vindictive killer of the Wild—but he would soon learn this lesson, too.

He was still whimpering when the mother-weasel reappeared. Now that her young one was safe, she did not rush him. She approached more cautiously, and the cub got a good look at her lean body with its eager, snakelike head. Her sharp, menacing cry sent the hair bristling along his back, and he snarled warningly at her. She came closer and closer, then leaped. Faster than he could follow, the lean yellow body disappeared briefly. The next moment she was at his throat, burying her teeth in his hair and flesh.

At first he snarled and tried to fight, but he

was very young, and this was only his first day in the outside world. His snarl became a whimper, his fight a struggle to escape. The weasel hung on, trying to reach the large vein in his neck. Like all weasels, she drank blood, and preferred to drink it from the throat of life itself.

The gray cub would have died, and there would have been no story to write about him, if the she-wolf had not come bounding through the bushes. The weasel let go of the cub and flashed at the she-wolf's throat, missing it, but getting a hold on her jaw, instead. The she-wolf snapped her head like a whip, breaking the weasel's hold and flinging it high in the air. As it fell, her jaws closed on the lean, yellow body, and the weasel died between the crunching teeth.

The cub received another burst of affection from his mother. Her joy at finding him seemed even greater than his joy at being found. She nuzzled him and licked the cuts made by the weasel's teeth. Then, together, mother and cub, they ate the blood-drinker. After that, they went back to the cave and slept.

CHAPTER FIVE
THE LAW OF MEAT

The cub developed rapidly. He rested for two days, then ventured out again. He found the young weasel and ate it, just as he had eaten its mother. But this time he did not get lost. When he grew tired, he found his way back to the cave and slept. Every day he traveled farther from the cave.

He began to know his strengths and his weaknesses, and to know when to be bold and when to be cautious. He found it best to be cautious all the time, except for rare moments when he lost control of himself. A stray grouse always sent him into a fury. He never failed to respond savagely to the chatter of the squirrel. The sight of a moose-bird almost always put him into a rage, for he never forgot that first peck on the nose.

But when he felt himself to be in danger from some other prowling meat hunter, not even a moose-bird bothered him. He never forgot the hawk, and its moving shadow always sent him crouching into the nearest bushes. He no longer sprawled awkwardly, and he was already developing his mother's walk, slinking, effortless, and deceptively swift.

His luck in hunting for meat had all come in the beginning. The seven grouse chicks and the baby weasel represented his only kills. More and more he wished to kill, hungering especially for the squirrel, whose chatter alerted everyone to his approach. But since the squirrel could climb trees, the cub could sneak up on it only when it was on the ground.

The cub greatly respected his mother. She could get meat, and she always brought him his share. Further, she was unafraid of things. He did not realize that this fearlessness came from experience and knowledge. But he was impressed with her power, which he came to know and respect. As he grew older, her temper grew shorter. Now she punished him with sharper paw-strokes and the slash of her fangs, rather than with nudges of the nose, as before. She required him to obey, and he respected her for this, as well.

Famine came again, and the cub was hungry. The she-wolf ran herself thin in the search for meat. She rarely slept in the cave, spending most of her time on the meat-trail without success. This famine was short, but severe. The cub found no more milk in his mother's breast, nor did he get one mouthful of meat.

Before, he had hunted in play, for the

sheer joyousness of it. Now it was serious, and he found nothing. But his failures taught him a lot. He studied every creature's habits carefully, trying to surprise or get at it. And there came a day when he did not run from the hawk's shadow. He had grown stronger and wiser, more confident—and hungry. In desperation he sat on his haunches in the open, challenging the hawk, which he knew to be the meat he craved. But the hawk refused to come down and fight, so the cub crawled away into a thicket and whimpered his disappointment and hunger.

The famine broke. Finally the she-wolf brought home meat. It was strange meat, different from any she had brought before. It was a lynx kitten, and it was all for him. He did not know that his mother had eaten the rest of the lynx litter. Nor did he know that this was a dangerous and desperate thing to do. He knew only that the velvet-furred kitten was meat, and he ate and grew happier with every mouthful. His belly now full, he slept against his mother's side.

He woke to her snarling. Possibly it was the most terrible snarl she ever gave. There was reason for it, and none knew it better than she. If you raided the lair of a lynx, you paid the price. In the full glare of the afternoon light, the cub saw the lynx-mother, crouching in the entrance to the cave. The hair rippled up his back in fear at the sight. He did not need instinct to be afraid of its snarling, hoarse screech of rage.

The cub felt life stir in him, and stood up and snarled valiantly by his mother's side. But she shoved him back. Because of the low-roofed entrance, the lynx had to crawl, rather than leap into the cave. When she did so, the she-wolf sprang upon her and pinned her down. The cub saw little of the battle. There was a lot of noise as the two animals thrashed about, the lynx ripping and tearing with her teeth and claws while the she-wolf used only her teeth.

Once, the cub sprang in and sank his teeth into the hind leg of the lynx. He held on, growling savagely, not realizing how much damage he saved his mother by hampering the leg. A change in the battle crushed him under both their bodies and broke his hold. The next moment, the two mothers separated. Then, before they rushed together again, the lynx lashed out at the cub with a huge forepaw, which ripped his shoulder open to the bone and sent him flying against the wall. His yelp of pain and fright became part of the racket. But the fight lasted so long that he had time to cry himself out and then had a second burst of courage. The end of the battle found him again clinging to a hind leg, growling furiously.

The lynx was dead. But the she-wolf was badly hurt and very weak. At first she caressed the cub and licked his wounded shoulder. But the bleeding had taken away her strength. For a day and a night, she lay beside the dead lynx, without movement and barely breathing. For a week she left the cave only for water, moving slowly and painfully. At the end of that time, the lynx was fully eaten, and the she-wolf's wounds had healed enough to permit her to continue on the meat-trail again.

The cub's shoulder was stiff and sore, and for some time he limped from the terrible slash he had received. But the world now seemed changed. He went about in it with greater confidence than in the days before the battle with the lynx. He had fought, buried his teeth in the flesh of an enemy, and survived. And because of all this, he carried himself with a new defiance. He was no longer afraid of minor things, though the unknown and its mysteries continued to terrify him.

He joined his mother on the meat-trail and learned the law of meat. There were two kinds of life. His own kind included his mother and himself. The other kind was divided into living things that he could kill and eat, and living things that could kill and eat him. There were the eaters and the eaten. Life was meat. Life lived on meat. Therefore, life lived on life. And so the law was, "eat or be eaten."

He did not think about this law the way a human might. He simply lived it, the same as the hawk, the grouse-mother and her chicks, and the lynx-mother and her kittens. He accepted his part in this world of living, eating, killing, and being killed. But living also included the thrill of hunting, the pleasure of napping in the sunshine, and even the terrifying mystery of the unknown. He was living his life fully. And so he was happy and very proud of himself.

PART THREE:
THE GODS OF THE WILD

CHAPTER ONE
THE MAKERS OF FIRE

The cub came upon it suddenly. It was his own fault. He had been careless. He was sleepy from being out all night on the meat-trail, and the trail to the pool was very familiar. Nothing had ever happened on it. He had simply left the cave and run carelessly down to the stream to drink.

He went down past the blasted pine, crossed the open space, and trotted in among the trees. Then, at the same instant, he saw and smelled them. Before him, sitting silently on their haunches, were five live things unlike any he had seen before. It was his first glimpse of mankind. But at the sight of him, they did not spring to their feet, nor show their teeth, nor snarl. They did not move, but sat there, silent and unknown.

The cub remained still, though every instinct would have told him to run wildly away. Another, greater instinct kept him motionless, one he felt for the first time—a great awe, a sense of his own weakness and littleness. His instinct told him that man was the animal that had won mastery over the other animals of the Wild. As countless ancestors had, he must fear and respect the animal who was lord over living things. A full-grown wolf would have run away, but the heritage was too strong for the cub, and he cowered down in submission and fear.

One of the Indians came to him, and leaned over him. The cub cowered closer to the ground. The unknown was now solid flesh and blood, reaching down to grab him. His hair bristled, his lips writhed back, and he bared his little fangs. The hand, poised above him, hesitated, and the man spoke, laughing, *"Wabam wabisca ip pit tah."* ("Look! The white fangs!")

The other Indians laughed loudly, and urged the man to pick up the cub. As the hand descended, two instincts battled within the cub—submit or fight. He did both. He submitted until the hand almost touched him. Then he fought, sinking his teeth into the hand. The next moment, he received a blow alongside his head, knocking him over and taking the fight out of him. Puppyhood and submission won, and he sat up on his haunches and *ki-yi*'d. But the man whose hand he had bitten was angry. He whacked the cub again on the head, making him sit up and *ki-yi* louder than ever.

The four Indians laughed more loudly, joined even by the bitten man—laughing at the cub while he wailed out his terror and his hurt. In the midst of it, he heard something. The Indians heard it too. But the cub recognized it, and with a last, long wail that became one of victory, he fell quiet and waited for his fearless mother. She was ferocious; she fought and killed all things. Snarling, she dashed in to save her cub.

She bounded in among them, in a mother's fury. The cub uttered a glad little cry and bounded to meet her, while the man-animals hastily went back several steps. The she-wolf stood over against her cub, facing the men, hair bristled, a snarl rumbling deep in her throat. Her face was so twisted with menace that it wrinkled the bridge of her nose.

Then it was that a cry went up from one of the men. "Kiche!" It was an exclamation of surprise. The cub felt his mother wilting at the sound.

"Kiche!" the man cried again, this time with sharp authority.

And then the cub was stunned and

dismayed to see his mother, the fearless she-wolf, crouching down, whimpering, and submitting. He could not understand. He was shocked. The awe of man rushed over him again. His instinct about them had been correct, for even his mother submitted to the man-animals.

The man who had spoken came over to her. He put his hand upon her head, but she only crouched closer. She did not snap, nor threaten to snap. The other men came up and surrounded her and touched her. She did not seem to resent them. They were greatly excited and made many noises with their mouths. As he crouched near his mother, still bristling from time to time but trying to submit, the cub decided that these were not dangerous noises.

"It is not strange," an Indian was saying. "Her father was a wolf. It is true, her mother was a dog. But did my brother not tie her out in the woods for three nights in the mating season? The father of Kiche was therefore a wolf."

"It is a year, Gray Beaver, since she ran away," spoke a second Indian.

"It is not strange, Salmon Tongue," Gray Beaver answered. "It was the time of the famine, and there was no meat for the dogs."

"She has lived with the wolves," said a third Indian.

"So it would seem, Three Eagles," Gray Beaver answered, laying his hand on the cub. "And this is proof of it."

The cub snarled a little at the touch, and the hand drew back to hit him. At this, the cub covered its fangs and sank down. The hand returned and rubbed behind his ears, and up and down his back.

"This be the sign of it," Gray Beaver went on. "It is plain that his mother is Kiche. But his father was a wolf. In him there is little dog and much wolf. His fangs be white, and White Fang shall be his name. I have spoken. He is my dog. For was not Kiche my brother's dog? And is not my brother dead?"

The cub, who had thus received a name in the world, lay and watched. For a time, the man-animals continued to make their mouth-noises. Then Gray Beaver took a knife, went into the thicket, and cut a stick. White Fang watched him. He notched the stick at each end, and in the notches fastened rawhide strings. He tied one string around the throat of Kiche, then led her to a small pine, around which he tied the other string.

White Fang followed and lay down beside her. Salmon Tongue's hand reached out to him and rolled him over on his back. Kiche looked on anxiously. White Fang felt fear mounting in him again, and he let out a snarl, but did not snap. The hand rubbed his stomach playfully, rolling him from side to side. It was ridiculous, lying there on his back with legs in the air in an utterly helpless position. It went against White Fang's whole nature to be so helpless. If this man-animal meant harm, White Fang knew that he could not escape it. Yet submission overcame his fear, and he only growled softly.

He could not suppress the growl, but the man-animal did not resent it by hitting him on the head. Even more strangely, White Fang felt an unexplainable sensation of pleasure. The hand rolled him on his side, scratched behind his ears. He stopped growling. With a final rub, the man went away, and White Fang felt no more fear for the moment. He would know fear many times in his future dealings with man, but, in the end, their companionship would be a fearless one.

After a time, White Fang heard strange noises approaching. He knew at once they were man-animal noises. A few minutes later the remainder of the tribe trailed in. There were more men, and many women and children, forty in all. They were heavily burdened with camp equipment. There were also many dogs, and except for the part-grown puppies, they, too, were loaded down heavily with camping gear.

White Fang had never seen dogs before. But at the sight of them, he felt that they were his own kind, only somehow different. But they displayed little difference from the wolf when they discovered the cub and his mother. There was a rush. White Fang bristled and snarled and snapped in the face of the open-mouthed, oncoming wave of dogs. He went down under them, feeling the sharp slash of teeth in his body, biting and tearing at the legs and bellies above him. There was a great uproar. He could hear Kiche snarl as she defended him. He could also could hear the cries of the man-animals, the sound of clubs striking upon bodies, and the yelps of pain from the dogs.

In a few seconds he was on his feet again. He could now see the man-animals driving the dogs back with clubs and stones, saving him from the savage teeth of his kind, who somehow were not his kind. He didn't really understand concepts like justice, but in his own way, he saw the man-animals as the powerful executors of justice and law. They neither bit nor clawed, but enforced their law with dead things. Dead things obeyed them, leaping like living things to give the dogs painful hurt. This was incredible power. He could only understand it as godlike, in the way that man would stand in awe of some god on a mountaintop, hurling thunderbolts at an astonished world.

The last dog had been driven back. The hubbub died down. White Fang licked his hurts and meditated on his first taste of the cruelty of the pack. He had never dreamed that his own kind consisted of more than One Eye, his mother, and himself. They had been one kind, and there were apparently many more creatures of this, his own kind. Deep down, he resented that their first act had been to try to destroy him. He also resented his mother's bondage, even though it was done by the superior man-animals. It felt like a trap. He had been free to roam or lie down at will, and now he was restricted. His mother could move no further than the length of a stick, and since he still needed to be near his mother's side, neither could he.

He did not like it. Nor did he like it when the man-animals resumed their march, for a tiny man-animal led Kiche by the stick. She trailed behind him, as a captive. White Fang followed, very worried about this new adventure.

They went down the valley, further than he had ever gone, to the place where the stream fed into the Mackenzie River. Here they camped. Canoes were stored on pole-frames high in the air, and there were drying-racks for fish. White Fang looked on with wonder. The man-animals became more superior with every moment. Their mastery over all these sharp-fanged dogs was power enough. But to him, greater still was their mastery over things not alive. They had the ability to move unmoving things, and to change the world.

This ability impressed him the most. He saw frames of poles go up, but this was not so strange, because it was done by the same creatures that could throw sticks and stones great distances. But when the frames of poles were made into tepees by being covered with cloth and skins, White Fang was astounded. They were huge and bulky, surrounding him on every side, looming frighteningly over him. When the wind stirred them, he watched the tepees warily, cowering in fear, ready to spring away if they somehow leaped on him.

But in a short while, this fear passed away. He saw the women and children passing in and out of them without harm. He also saw the dogs trying often to enter them, and being driven away with sharp words and flying stones. After a time, he left Kiche's side and crawled cautiously toward the wall of the nearest tepee, urged on by the curiosity of growth.

He crawled the last few inches with painfully slow caution. Awesome, unknown things had happened today. At last his nose touched the canvas. He waited. Nothing happened. Then he smelled the strange fabric, full of the man-smell. He gave the canvas a gentle tug with his teeth. Nothing happened, though the adjacent portions of the tepee moved. He tugged harder. There was a greater movement. It was delightful. He tugged still harder over and over until he shook the whole tepee. Then the sharp cry of a woman inside sent him scampering back to Kiche. But after that, he no longer feared the looming tepees.

A moment later he was straying again from his mother, who was still tied up. A part-grown puppy, somewhat larger and older than he, came slowly toward him. He acted aggressive and important. The puppy's name, as White Fang would later learn, was Lip-lip. He had had experience in puppy fights and was already something of a bully.

Lip-lip was White Fang's own kind, and,

being only a puppy, did not seem dangerous. So White Fang prepared to meet him as a friend. But when the stranger's walk became stiff-legged and he bared his teeth, White Fang stiffened and bared his own. They half circled each other, hesitantly, snarling and bristling. This lasted several minutes, and White Fang was beginning to enjoy it, as a sort of game. But suddenly, with amazing swiftness, Lip-lip leaped in and delivered a slashing snap, then leaped away again. The snap had hit the shoulder that was still sore from the lynx's claws. First he yelped in surprise, but in the next moment White Fang felt a rush of anger and leaped on Lip-lip, snapping viciously.

But Lip-lip was a veteran of many puppy fights in camp. His sharp little teeth scored half a dozen hits on the newcomer, until White Fang, yelping shamelessly, fled to the protection of his mother. It was the first of many fights he was to have with Lip-lip, for they were born to be enemies.

Kiche licked White Fang soothingly with her tongue, and tried to convince him to remain with her. But he was very curious, and several minutes later he was away on a new adventure. He came upon one of the man-animals, Gray Beaver, who was squatting on the ground and doing something with sticks and dry moss spread before him. White Fang came near to him and watched.

Women and children were carrying more sticks and branches to Gray Beaver. It seemed like an important moment. White Fang was so curious that he touched Gray Beaver's knee, forgetting that this was a terrible man-animal. Suddenly he saw a strange thing, like mist, arise from the sticks and moss. Then, among the sticks themselves, appeared a live thing, twisting and turning, looking like the sun in the sky. White Fang knew nothing about fire. It drew him as the light in the mouth of the cave had attracted him in his early puppyhood. He crawled toward the flame. He heard Gray Beaver chuckle above him, but this time the sound was not hostile. Then his nose touched the flame, and at the same instant his little tongue went out to it.

For a moment he was paralyzed. The unknown, lurking in the sticks and moss, was savagely clutching him by the nose. He scrambled backward, letting out a burst of *ki-yi*'s. Snarling, Kiche leaped to the end of her stick, raging terribly because she could not come to his aid. But Gray Beaver laughed loudly, and slapped his thighs, and told the rest of the camp about it, until everybody was laughing noisily. But White Fang sat on his haunches and *ki-yi*'d, a miserable, lonely little figure in the midst of the man-animals.

It was the worst hurt he had ever known. The live, sun-colored thing that had grown up under Gray Beaver's hands had scorched his nose and tongue. He cried and cried, every fresh wail bringing more laughter from the man-animals. He tried to soothe his nose with his tongue, but it was burned, too, and the two hurts coming together produced greater hurt. He cried more hopelessly and helplessly than ever.

Then he felt shame. He knew what laughter meant. That he was being laughed at by the man-animals made him ashamed. White Fang turned and fled, not from the hurt of the fire, but from the laughter that so deeply hurt his spirit. He fled to Kiche, who was raging madly at the end of her stick—to the one creature in the world who was not laughing at him.

Twilight faded into night, and White Fang lay by his mother's side. His nose and tongue still hurt, but he was perplexed by a greater trouble. He was homesick. He missed the peace and quiet of the stream and the cliff-cave. There was too much life around, too many man-animals of all types, all making irritating noises. And there were the dogs, always bickering,

constantly and noisily active. The restful loneliness of the only life he had known was gone.
Here the very air was full of life, humming
and buzzing, constantly changing. It made
him too nervous to rest, for fear that something might happen.

He watched the man-animals moving
about the camp. He saw them as divine, superior, working wonders. They had unknown
powers, ruled things alive and things not
alive, and made everything move and obey.
They made sun-colored life out of dead moss
and wood. They were fire-makers! They were
gods.

CHAPTER TWO
THE BONDAGE

The days were full of new experiences for White Fang. While Kiche was tied to the stick, he ran all over the camp, investigating and learning. The more he came to know the man-animals, the more superior and godlike they seemed.

Man has often grieved to see his gods and altars overthrown, but the wolf and the wild dog—who crouch before man—have never known this grief. Man's gods often reflect man himself and his desires. In order to believe in them, one must have faith. But the god of the wolf and the wild dog is of solid flesh, and requires no faith. It stands on its two hind legs, an intense mix of power and passion and mystery, and carries a club. Yet this god is wrapped in flesh and blood, which—like any meat—is also good to eat.

And so it was with White Fang. The man-animals were certainly gods that could not be escaped. As his mother had surrendered to them, so he was beginning to respect their rule. He got out of their way. When they called, he came. When they threatened, he cowered. When they commanded him to go, he hurried away. Their every wish was enforced with powerful hurt in the form of clubs, flying stones, and the lash of whips.

He belonged to them as all dogs belonged to them. His actions were theirs to command. He quickly learned that his body was theirs to maul or to tolerate. This was against much of his own strong, dominant nature. It was an unpleasant learning process, but he learned to like dependence. It was easier when the responsibilities of life were shifted onto someone else. But it did not happen all at once. His heritage and memories of the Wild remained. Some days he crept to the edge of the forest and listened to something calling him away. But he always returned, restless and uncomfortable, to whimper softly at Kiche's side and to lick her face with an eager, questioning tongue.

White Fang rapidly learned the ways of camp. He knew the injustice and greed of the older dogs when meat or fish was thrown out to be eaten. He came to know that men were more fair, children more cruel, and women more kindly and more likely to toss him a bit of meat or bone. And after two or three painful adventures with the mothers of part-grown puppies, he learned that it was always wise to avoid them.

But the worst thing in his life was Lip-lip.

Larger, older, and stronger, Lip-lip made White Fang the victim of his bullying. White Fang fought willingly enough, but his enemy was too big. Lip-lip became his nightmare. Whenever White Fang ventured away from his mother, the bully was sure to appear, trailing at his heels and snarling. If no man-animal was near, he would start a fight. Since Lip-lip always won, he enjoyed it hugely. His chief delight in life became White Fang's chief torment.

But even though White Fang always got the worst of the fights, he was not humbled. His spirit remained strong, but he became distant and mean. He had inherited a savage temper, and this endless cruelty made it more savage. He never frolicked with the other puppies, as a normal puppy would do. If White Fang came near them, Lip-lip showed up to bully him away.

The effect of this was to rob White Fang of much of his puppyhood. He grew up quickly, using his energy to become trickier and more cunning, rather than to romp with the others. When the dogs were fed, they kept him from getting his share, so he became a clever thief. He learned to fend for himself, to the annoyance of the women of the camp. He sneaked about camp, was constantly on the alert, and figured out many ways to avoid the bully.

It was early in the days of his torment that White Fang played his first really big, crafty game and got his first taste of revenge. As Kiche had once lured dogs out from men's camps to their deaths, White Fang lured Lip-lip into Kiche's avenging jaws.

Retreating before Lip-lip one day, White Fang took off on a random course through the tepees. He was the fastest puppy in camp for his size, faster than Lip-lip, but he paced himself to stay just one leap ahead. Lip-lip was too excited by the chase to remember where they were going. By the time he did, it was too late. Dashing at top speed around a tepee, he ran full tilt into Kiche lying at the end of her stick. He yelped once, and then her punishing jaws closed upon him. She was tied, but he could not get away from her easily. She rolled him off his legs so that he could not run, then repeatedly ripped and slashed him with her fangs.

When he finally rolled clear of her, he crawled to his feet, badly disheveled. Both his body and spirit were both hurt. His hair stood out all over him in tufts where her teeth had mauled. He opened his mouth to let forth a long, broken-hearted puppy wail, but in the middle of it, White Fang rushed in and sank his teeth into Lip-lip's hind leg. There was no fight left in Lip-lip, and he ran away shamelessly to his own tepee, with White Fang like a raging demon on his heels. At the tepee the women came to his aid, finally driving White Fang off with a volley of thrown rocks.

One day Gray Beaver decided that Kiche was no longer likely to run away, so he released her. White Fang was delighted. He accompanied her joyfully about the camp, and as long as he stayed close by her side, Lip-lip kept a respectful distance. White Fang even bristled up to him, trying to provoke him, but Lip-lip ignored the challenge. He was no fool, and his revenge could wait until he caught White Fang alone.

Later on that day, Kiche and White Fang strayed into the edge of the woods next to the camp. He had led his mother there, step by step. When she stopped, he tried to encourage her farther. The stream, the lair, and the quiet woods were calling to him. He ran on a few steps, stopped, and looked back. She did not move. He whined pleadingly, ducking playfully in and out of the underbrush. He ran back to her, licked her face, and ran on again. Still she did not move. He stopped and looked at her, and the eagerness drained out of him as she turned to gaze back at the camp.

There was something calling to him out there. His mother heard it, too. But she also heard a louder call—that of the fire and of man, the call that only the wolf and the wild dog may answer.

Kiche turned and slowly trotted back toward camp. The camp, with its gods, held her more strongly than the stick. White Fang sat down and whimpered softly. A strong smell of pine reminded him of his old life of freedom, but he was still a puppy, and his mother's call was stronger than that of the Wild. The time had not yet come for his independence. So he arose and trotted sadly back to camp, pausing once and twice to whimper and listen to the call that still sounded in the depths of the forest.

A mother's time with her young in the Wild is short enough, but it can be even shorter when man is in control. Gray Beaver was in debt to Three Eagles, who was going away on a trip up the Mackenzie River. Kiche was used to pay off his debt. White Fang saw his mother taken aboard Three Eagles' canoe, and tried to follow her. A blow from Three Eagles knocked him back to the land. The canoe shoved off. White Fang sprang into the water and swam after it, deaf to the sharp cries of Gray Beaver. White Fang ignored a man-animal—a god—so strong was his terror of losing his mother.

But gods are used to being obeyed, and Gray Beaver angrily launched a canoe in pursuit. When he overtook White Fang, he reached down and yanked him out of the water. Holding him by the nape of the neck, he gave White Fang a beating. And it was a harsh beating. His hand was heavy. Every blow was meant to hurt, and he delivered many blows. White Fang swung back and forth. First he felt surprise, then fear, and finally anger. He snarled fearlessly in the face of the angry god, but this made the god angrier, and the beating got even worse.

Gray Beaver continued to beat, and White Fang continued to snarl. But this could not last forever. Someone had to give up, and it was White Fang. Fear surged through him. This was a real man-handling, one that made thrown sticks and stones seem gentle. He broke down and began to cry and yelp. His fear turned into terror until his yelps went on without stopping.

At last Gray Beaver stopped. White Fang, hanging limply, continued to cry. This seemed to satisfy his master, who flung him down roughly in the bottom of the canoe. Gray

Beaver picked up the paddle. White Fang was in his way. He shoved him savagely aside with his foot. In that moment, White Fang's free nature came out again, and he sank his teeth through the leather moccasin and into the foot.

The pounding he now received made the earlier beating look mild. Gray Beaver was as infuriated as White Fang was afraid. He hammered him with both his hand and the hard wooden paddle. When White Fang was flung again into the bottom of the canoe, his whole body was bruised and sore. Gray Beaver purposefully kicked him again, and this time White Fang did not bite. He had learned a lesson of bondage. He must never dare to bite his god, his master. That was the worst crime, one that would never be overlooked.

When the canoe touched the shore, White Fang lay still, whimpering and motionless, waiting. Gray Beaver flung him ashore, where he landed heavily on his bruised side. He crawled, trembling, to his feet and stood whimpering. Lip-lip, who had watched the whole affair from the bank, now rushed upon him, knocking him over and biting him.

White Fang was too helpless to defend himself. He would have been badly hurt. But Gray Beaver's foot shot out, lifting Lip-lip into the air so far that he smashed down to earth a dozen feet away. This was the man-animal's justice. Even then, in his own misery, White Fang experienced a little grateful thrill. At Gray Beaver's heels, he limped obediently through the village to the tepee. And so White Fang learned that the right to punish was something reserved only for the gods.

That night, when all was still, White Fang remembered his mother and cried sorrowfully for her. He wept too loudly and woke up Gray Beaver, who beat him. After that he mourned gently when the gods were around. But sometimes, straying off to the edge of the woods by himself, he wailed out his grief loudly. During this time, he might have run back to the Wild, but the memory of his mother held him. After all, the hunting man-animals went out and came back. She, too, might return someday, so he remained in bondage and waited for her.

But his bondage was not completely unhappy. There was always something interesting happening. There was no end to the strange things these gods did, and he was always curious to see them. Besides, he was learning how to get along with Gray Beaver. Rigid obedience was required of him, and in return he escaped beatings and was tolerated.

Sometimes, Gray Beaver even tossed him a piece of meat, and defended his right to eat it against the other dogs' bullying. Such a piece of meat was, in some strange way, worth more than a dozen such pieces from a woman's hand. Gray Beaver never petted nor caressed. Perhaps it was the justice or the sheer power of him that influenced White Fang, but a sense of attachment was forming between him and his lord.

In subtle as well as obvious ways, the shackles of White Fang's bondage were tightened upon him. The qualities that had made it possible for wolves and wild dogs to come in to men's fires in the first place were developed further by life in camp. Without knowing it, and despite its many miseries, a part of him was becoming attached to camp-life. But on the surface, he knew only grief for the loss of Kiche. He hoped for her return, and he hungered for the freedom that he had known.

CHAPTER THREE
THE OUTCAST

Lip-lip continued to make White Fang miserable. White Fang's heritage was already savage and fierce, and the abuse made him even more so. Even the man-animals began to consider him wicked. If there was an uproar in camp, a fight, or a woman yelling over stolen meat, they were sure to find White Fang mixed up in it. They didn't care about the cause of his conduct, just the results. He was a sneak, a thief, and a troublemaker. Angry women, whom he watched carefully to avoid thrown rocks, called him a worthless wolf and said that he would come to an evil end.

He found himself an outcast in the crowded camp. All the young dogs followed Lip-lip's lead. White Fang was different from them. Perhaps they sensed his wildness, and disliked him as the domestic dog dislikes the wolf. In any case, they joined Lip-lip in endlessly bullying him. They all also eventually felt his teeth, and he gave more than he received. One on one, he could whip many of them, but they never fought him alone. If a fight started, the rest of the young dogs quickly ganged up on him. Out of this he learned two important things: how to take care of himself in a gang-fight, and how to inflict the greatest amount of damage on a single dog in the briefest amount of time. The key to staying alive was to stay on his feet. Almost like a cat, he learned to keep his feet under him, even when knocked over by grown dogs.

When dogs fight, it usually begins with snarling and bristling and stiff-legged strutting. But White Fang learned that if he did this, the whole gang came. So he developed the habit of attacking without warning. He would rush in, snap and slash when his enemy was off guard, and then get away very quickly. A surprised dog, with its ear or shoulder wounded, was already half beaten. Surprise also made it easy to roll a dog over, which usually exposed the soft underside of its neck. He knew instinctively that this was where you struck in order to take a life. So his method became to surprise a young dog alone, knock it over, and go for its soft throat.

Being only partly grown, his jaws were not yet strong enough for his throat-attacks to kill, but they did leave many a young dog with a badly cut neck. And one day, catching one of his enemies alone on the edge of the woods, he managed, by repeatedly overthrowing him and attacking the throat, to cut the great vein and let out the life.

There was a big uproar that night. Witnesses had told the dead dog's master, and the women remembered all the meat that White Fang had swiped. Many people came angrily to Gray Beaver's tepee, complaining that enough was enough. But he had placed White Fang inside, and stubbornly held the door shut. He refused his tribespeople their revenge.

White Fang became hated by man and dog. As he grew, he never knew a moment's safety. The tooth of every dog was against him, the hand of every man. His own kind greeted him only with snarls. His gods greeted him with curses and stones. He lived tensely, on constant alert for sudden attacks. He was always prepared to dodge thrown objects, to leap away with a menacing snarl, or to counterattack with a flash of teeth.

He learned to snarl more terribly than any dog in camp, young or old. The intent of the snarl is to warn or frighten, and White Fang developed it to a fine art. His snarl contained all that was vicious, spiteful, and horrible. His nose would rumple, his hair would bristle, his tongue would whip out like a snake's. His ears flattened down, his eyes gleamed hatred, his lips curled back, and his fangs dripped. This was enough to make almost any attacker hesitate, and that temporary pause gave him a vital moment in which to decide what to do. However, the pause often lengthened into second thoughts about the attack. More than once, when White Fang faced one of the grown dogs, his snarl enabled him to make an honorable retreat.

The pack paid for its harassment of White Fang. By making him an outcast, they created a situation in which they could never safely be by themselves. His ambush tactics made the young dogs afraid to stray from the pack. Except for Lip-lip, they were forced to huddle together for protection against the terrible enemy they had made. A puppy alone by the riverbank would stir up the whole camp with its cry of pain and terror as it fled from White Fang—if it survived.

Even after the young dogs had learned to stay together, White Fang kept attacking. It was a state of war. He attacked them when he caught them alone, and they attacked him when they were in the pack. They chased him on sight. He could usually outrun them, but grief came to the dog that got too far out ahead of the pack. White Fang had learned to turn suddenly upon the pursuer, and thoroughly rip him up before the pack could arrive. This happened a lot, because the dogs tended to forget themselves in the excitement of the chase, while White Fang stayed focused. Stealing backward glances as he ran, he was always ready to whirl around and take down any dog that outran his fellows.

Young dogs are bound to play, and the hunting of White Fang became their chief game—but it was a deadly serious game. As the fastest runner, he was not afraid to venture anywhere. While he waited in vain for his mother to come back, he led the pack on many wild chases through the nearby woods. But the pack always lost him. Its noise warned him of its presence, while he ran alone, velvet-footed, silently, a moving shadow among the trees like his father and mother before him. He was also more directly connected with the Wild than the others. He knew more of its secrets and strategies. A favorite trick of his was to lose his trail in running water, then lie quietly in a nearby thicket while they ran around in confusion.

Hated by his own kind and by mankind, constantly at war, White Fang developed rapidly and one-sidedly. There was no room for kindness and affection; he had no concept of them. The code he learned was to obey the strong and oppress the weak. Gray Beaver was a god, and strong. Therefore, White Fang obeyed him. But a younger or smaller dog was weak, a thing to be destroyed. White Fang's development centered around power. In order to face the constant danger of hurt and destruction, he became a highly developed predator. He became quicker, craftier, deadlier, leaner, and stronger. He was more cruel and ferocious and had better endurance than the others. He was more intelligent. He had to become all these things, or he would not have survived.

CHAPTER FOUR
THE TRAIL OF THE GODS

In the fall, with the bite of the frost coming into the air, White Fang got his chance for freedom. For several days there had been a great hubbub in the village. The summer camp was being dismantled, and the tribe was packing up for fall hunting. White Fang watched it all with eager eyes, and when the tepees began to come down and the canoes were being loaded, he understood. Some canoes had already disappeared down the river.

Quite deliberately, he decided to stay behind. He waited for his opportunity to slink out of camp into the woods. Here in the running stream, he hid his trail. Then he crawled into the heart of the dense forest and waited. Dozing off now and then, he was wakened by Gray Beaver's voice calling his name. There were other voices. He could hear Gray Beaver's wife, and his son, Mit-sah, taking part in the search.

White Fang trembled with fear, but resisted the urge to crawl out of his hiding-place. After a time the voices died away, and some time later he crept out to enjoy his success. Darkness was coming on, and for a while he played among the trees, enjoying his freedom. Then, quite suddenly, he became aware of loneliness, and sat down to consider this. The forest felt ominously silent, with looming trees and dark shadows where danger could hide.

Then it was cold. There was no warm tepee to snuggle against. The frost was in his feet, and he kept lifting first one forefoot and then the other. He curved his bushy tail around to cover them, and at the same time he saw a vision, a series of images from his memory. He saw the camp, the tepees, the blazing fires. He heard the shrill voices of women, the deeper ones of the men, and the snarling of the dogs. He was hungry, and he remembered the food that people had given him.

Here there was no meat, nothing but a threatening silence. He had become soft in the camp. He had forgotten how to fend for himself. His senses, accustomed to the constant sights and sounds of camp, were now left idle. No matter how hard he tried, there was nothing to see or hear. The lack of action felt ominous to White Fang, as if something terrible were going to happen.

He gave a great start of fright. Something huge and shapeless was rushing across the field of his vision. It was just a tree-shadow flung by the moon as the clouds uncovered it. He was reassured and whimpered softly. But then he stopped, fearful of attracting the lurking dangers.

On cool autumn nights, trees sometimes cracked as the water in them froze. One such tree made a loud noise right above White Fang. He yelped with fright and fled in terrified panic toward the village. He felt an overpowering desire for the protection and friendship of man. He could smell the camp smoke, hear the camp cries. Bursting from the forest into the open, though, he saw that there was no village. He had forgotten. There was no place to flee to find comfort.

He slunk forlornly through the deserted camp, smelling the trash-heaps and the discarded rags and tags of the gods. He would have been glad to have an angry woman throw stones at him, or to have the hand of Gray Beaver angrily punish him. He would have welcomed even Lip-lip and the whole snarling, cowardly pack.

He came to the place where Gray Beaver's tepee had stood. In the center of the space it had occupied, he sat down. He pointed his nose at the moon and cried. Out poured his loneliness and fear, his grief for Kiche, all his past sorrows and miseries, as well as his fear of sufferings and dangers to come. It was the long wolf-howl, full-throated and mournful, the first howl he ever uttered.

The coming of daylight chased away his fears, but made him even lonelier. The earth was naked. There was no one. It did not take him long to make up his mind. He plunged into the forest and followed the riverbank down the stream. He ran all day without rest, as though made to run forever. And even when he was tired, his heritage of endurance gave him the strength to force his complaining body onward.

Where the river swung in against steep cliffs, he climbed the high mountains behind. He crossed rivers and streams that entered the main river. Sometimes he walked on the rim-ice that was forming, and sometimes he fell through it, struggling for life in the icy current. He was always on the lookout for the place where the trail of the gods might leave the river and proceed inland.

White Fang was smarter than most wolves, but his mind did not grasp the other bank of the Mackenzie. What if the trail of the gods led out on that side? It never entered his head. Later on, when he had traveled more and was wiser about trails and rivers, he might be able to grasp such a possibility, but not yet. Right now he ran blindly, considering only his own bank of the great river.

All night he pressed on, blundering into obstacles in the darkness. By the middle of the second day, he had been running for thirty hours straight, and the iron of his flesh was giving out. But the endurance of his mind kept him going. He had not eaten in forty hours, and he was weak with hunger. The repeated drenchings in the icy water hadn't helped. His handsome coat was muddy. The broad pads of his feet were bruised and bleeding, and his limp increased with the hours. To make it worse, snow was beginning to cover up the ground, making it slippery and difficult to find his way.

Gray Beaver had intended to camp that night on the far bank of the Mackenzie, for it was in the direction of the hunting. But on the near bank, shortly before dark, his wife Klookooch had spotted a moose coming down to drink. In a fortunate sequence of events for White Fang, Gray Beaver had killed it with a lucky rifle shot, so they camped on the near side of the Mackenzie. Had they not, White Fang would have passed by without finding them, and either died or joined his wild brothers and become a wolf.

Night had fallen. The snow was flying more thickly, and White Fang, whimpering softly to himself as he stumbled and limped along, came upon a fresh trail in the snow. It was so fresh that he knew immediately what it was. Whining eagerly, he followed it back from the riverbank into the trees. The camp-sounds came to his ears. He saw the blaze of the fire, Kloo-kooch cooking, and Gray Beaver squatting on his hams and chewing a chunk of raw fat. There was fresh meat in camp!

White Fang expected a beating. He crouched and bristled a little at the thought of it. Then he went forward again. He wasn't looking forward to the punishment he knew to be waiting for him. But he knew other things came with it—the protection of the gods, the companionship of the dogs. Even having his enemies around was better than being alone.

He came cringing and crawling into the firelight. Gray Beaver saw him, and stopped munching the piece of hardened fat. White Fang crawled slowly toward him in total submission. He chose to surrender his body and soul. He came in to sit by man's fire and be ruled by him. Gray Beaver's hand moved above him. White Fang trembled, expecting punishment, but there was no blow. Gray Beaver was breaking the lump of fat in half to share with him! White Fang first sniffed and then began to eat the tallow. Gray Beaver ordered meat to be brought to him and guarded him from the other dogs while he ate.

After that, grateful and content, White Fang lay at Gray Beaver's feet, gazing at the fire that warmed him, blinking and dozing. He was secure in the knowledge that tomorrow would find him, not wandering alone through bleak forests, but in the camp of the man-animals, the gods—on whom he was now dependent.

CHAPTER FIVE
THE COVENANT

Well into December, Gray Beaver went on a journey up the Mackenzie. Mit-sah and Kloo-kooch went with him, using two dogsleds. He drove one sled himself, drawn by dogs he had traded for or borrowed. A second and smaller sled was driven by Mit-sah, drawn by a team of puppies. It was more of a toy affair than anything else, yet it delighted Mit-sah, who felt that he was beginning to do a man's work. His sled carried nearly two hundred pounds of supplies. Also, he was learning to train and drive dogs, while the puppies themselves were getting used to the harness.

White Fang had seen the camp-dogs working in the harness, so he did not resent it much when they first placed the harness on him. A collar was put about his neck, connected by two pulling-traces to a strap that passed around his chest and over his back. This was fastened to the sled with a long rope.

There were seven puppies in the team. The others were a month or two older than White Fang. Each dog was fastened to the sled by a single rope. No two ropes were of the same length, while the difference in length between any two ropes was at least that of a dog's body. Every rope attached to a ring at the front end of the sled. The sled itself was flat-bottomed with an upturned forward end to keep it from plowing under the soft snow.

The dogs at the ends of their ropes ran in a fan-shape ahead of the nose of the sled, so that no dog marched in another's footsteps. The formation also prevented the dogs from attacking those in front of them. The more a dog tried to catch those ahead of him, the harder he pulled the sled and the faster it moved, even though he never caught the dog. The Indians knew how to use the dogs' natural tendencies to keep them under control and to keep the sled moving.

Mit-sah looked like his father and had much of his wisdom. In the past he had noticed Lip-lip's cruelty to White Fang. But at that time Lip-lip was another man's dog, and Mit-sah had never dared do more than throw an occasional stone at him. But now Lip-lip was his dog, and Mit-sah got revenge on Lip-lip by putting him at the end of the longest rope.

This made Lip-lip the leader, which looked like an honor, but in reality was the opposite. Instead of being the bully and leader, he now found himself hated and

picked on by the pack. The dogs' view of him was always that of his tail end running away in front of them, which was a lot less frightening than his bristling mane and fangs. And dogs instinctively want to chase any dog that seems to be running away from them.

The moment the sled started, the team began an all-day chase after Lip-lip. At first he had turned upon his pursuers, furious and indignant. But at such times Mit-sah would give him a stinging lash in the face with his thirty-foot whip. Lip-lip was willing to face the pack, but not that whip, so all he could do was to keep his rope tight and his flanks away from the other dogs.

But Mit-sah was even more cunning. He favored the leader, giving meat only to him, which drove the others mad with jealousy and hatred. They would rage just out of whip-range, while Lip-lip devoured the meat. And when there was no meat, Mit-sah would keep the team at a distance and pretend to feed Lip-lip. This made them even more eager to catch him.

White Fang liked the work well enough. More than the other dogs, he had come to accept the rule of the gods, and he knew better than they how useless it was to resist. In addition, the persecution he had suffered from the pack made them less important to him, and man more important. He did not look to his own kind for friends. Kiche was nearly forgotten, so the chief way for him to express himself was through loyalty to his masters, the gods. So he worked hard, learned discipline, and obeyed, for these are instincts that wolves and wild dogs show when they have been tamed by man.

A kind of companionship did exist between White Fang and the other dogs, but it was one of warfare and hostility. He had never learned to play with them. He knew only how to fight, and this he did, paying them back a hundred times for every snap and slash they had given him when Lip-lip had been pack leader. But Lip-lip was no longer leader—except when he fled before his mates at the end of his rope, with the sled bounding along behind. In camp Lip-lip kept close to Mit-sah or Gray Beaver or Kloo-kooch. He did not dare venture away from the gods, for now the fangs of all dogs were against him, and Lip-lip felt the same persecution that White Fang had.

With the overthrow of Lip-lip, White Fang could have become leader of the pack, but he was too bad-tempered and solitary for that. When he wasn't beating up his teammates, he ignored them, and they kept out of his way and away from his meat. In fact, they ate their own meat quickly, afraid he would steal it from them. White Fang knew the law well: oppress the weak and obey the strong. He ate his share of meat as rapidly as he could. Then if any dog had not yet finished his own, there would be a snarl and a flash of fangs, and that dog would wail his annoyance to the uncomforting stars while White Fang finished his dinner for him.

Every little while, however, one dog or another would resist White Fang and be promptly subdued. In this way, White Fang was kept in training. In order to remain isolated while in the pack, he fought often, but the fights were brief. White Fang was so quick that any dog who rebelled was slashed and bleeding before he knew it. His discipline of the others was as rigid as the sled-discipline of the gods, forcing them to show him respect. They could do as they liked among themselves, as long as they did not challenge him or get in his way. If they showed him the faintest hint of stiff-leggedness, or lifted a lip, or bristled, he was on them immediately to show them the error of their ways.

He was a monstrous tyrant. The harsh struggles of his cubhood alongside his mother, fighting to survive in the Wild, had taught him to be ferocious. And he had also learned to respect superior strength. During the journey with Gray Beaver, when they came into strange man-animals' camps where there were full-grown dogs, he walked lightly among them.

The months passed, and the journey continued. The long hours on the trail and the steady work pulling the sled made White Fang stronger. He had come to know well the world in which he lived. His outlook was bleak and greedy. His world was fierce and brutal, lacking warmth or kindness of heart. He had no affection for Gray Beaver. True, he was a god, but a most savage god. White Fang acknowledged his lordship based on his superior intelligence and brute strength.

Something in White Fang made him desire this lordship, or else he would not have returned to the fire from the Wild. The part of him that might have learned to respond to a kind word and a gentle caress never grew, because those were not Gray Beaver's ways. Gray Beaver's law was the savage one of the club. He punished sins with the pain of a blow and rewarded good behavior not by kindness, but by withholding a blow.

So White Fang knew nothing of the joy a man's hand might give him. Besides, he did not trust the hands of the man-animals. True, they sometimes gave meat, but more often they gave hurt. Hands were things to avoid. They hurled stones, wielded sticks and clubs and whips, and were most likely to hurt him. In strange villages he had found that the children's hands also gave hurt. He had once nearly had an eye poked out by a toddling child, and so he was suspicious of all children and avoided them.

It was in a village at the Great Slave Lake that he learned something new. Before this, Gray Beaver's law dictated that to bite a god was the unpardonable crime. In this village, like all dogs in all villages, White Fang went scrounging for food. A boy was chopping frozen moose-meat with an axe, and the meat-chips were flying in the snow. White Fang, sliding by in quest of meat, stopped and began to eat the chips. He saw the boy put down the axe and pick up a stout club. White Fang sprang clear, just in time to escape the blow. The boy chased him, and he fled between two tepees to find himself cornered against a high earth bank in the strange village.

The boy guarded White Fang's only escape route. Holding his club ready to strike, the boy advanced on his cornered quarry. White Fang was furious. He faced the boy, bristling and snarling, his sense of justice outraged. He knew the law of foraging for food. All wasted meat, such as the frozen chips, belonged to the dog that found it. He had done no wrong, yet here was this boy preparing to beat him. Before he or the boy knew it, a surge of rage went through White Fang, and the boy was knocked over in the snow, his club-hand ripped wide open.

But White Fang knew that he had broken the law of the gods. He had driven his teeth into the flesh of one of them, and he could expect terrible punishment. He fled away to Gray Beaver, behind whom he crouched when the bitten boy and his family came.

They demanded vengeance, but they didn't get it. Gray Beaver defended White Fang. So did Mit-sah and Kloo-kooch. White Fang, listening to the argument and watching the angry gestures, knew that his act was justified. And so he learned that there were different kinds of gods. From his own gods, he had to take what he got, fair or unfair. But he was not required to take injustice from the other gods. It was his privilege to resist it with his teeth. And this also was a law of the gods.

Before the day was out, White Fang learned more about this law. When Mit-sah was alone, gathering firewood in the forest, he ran into the boy that had been bitten and some of his friends. After some angry words, all the boys attacked Mit-sah, and he was getting beaten up. At first White Fang just watched. This was an affair of the gods, and no concern of his. Then he realized that this was Mit-sah, one of his own particular gods, being mistreated. He felt another mad rush of anger, and leaped into the battle. Soon the landscape was covered with fleeing boys, many bleeding from his bites. When Mit-sah told the story in camp, Gray Beaver ordered extra meat to be given to White Fang. Dozing by the fire, belly full, White Fang understood the new law.

At the same time, White Fang came to learn the law of defense of property. He made the step from protecting his god's body to the protecting his god's things from theft. They were to be defended even if it meant biting other gods. Such an act was full of danger, because no dog was a match for the gods, yet White Fang learned to face them, fierce and unafraid. Duty rose above fear, and thieving gods learned to leave Gray Beaver's property alone.

In connection with this, White Fang quickly learned to give an alarm, not by barking—which he never did—but by charging and biting. He found that a thieving god was usually a coward, likely to run away if the alarm was given. He also learned that soon after he sounded this alarm, Gray Beaver showed up very quickly. Having nothing to do with other dogs, White Fang was perfect for guarding his master's property, and Gray Beaver encouraged him. So White Fang grew more ferocious and solitary.

The months went by, binding dog and man more and more strongly in their ancient covenant—this agreement that started with the first wolf who ever came in from the Wild. And like all wolves and wild dogs before him, White Fang understood this agreement's simple terms. He traded in his liberty and was possessed by a flesh-and-blood god. He received food and fire, protection and companionship. In return, he guarded the god's property, defended his body, worked for him, and obeyed him.

White Fang's service was one of duty and awe, but not of love. He did not know what love was. Kiche was a remote memory. He had abandoned the Wild when he gave himself up to man. And besides, even if he met Kiche again, the terms of the agreement would not allow him to desert his god to go with her. His loyalty to man was more important than his love of liberty, his kind, and his family.

CHAPTER SIX
THE FAMINE

Gray Beaver finished his long journey in April, and White Fang was a year old when he pulled into the home village and was unharnessed by Mit-sah. Though nowhere near fully grown, White Fang was the largest yearling in the village except for Lip-lip. He inherited good size from his wolf father and from Kiche. Already he was measuring up alongside the full-grown dogs. He was still filling out, his young body slender and stringy, not yet massive. His coat and overall look were those of a full-blooded wolf, though his one-fourth-dog blood from Kiche influenced his mental makeup.

He wandered through the village, recognizing with satisfaction the various gods he had known before the long journey. Then there were the dogs—puppies growing up like him, and grown dogs that did not look as big and dangerous as he remembered. He walked among them with less fear than before, and with a certain careless ease.

One of them was Baseek, a grizzled old fellow. In White Fang's younger days, Baseek only had to uncover his fangs to send White Fang cringing away. From him, White Fang had learned how small and powerless he was.

From Baseek he would soon learn how much stronger he had grown.

It happened when a freshly killed moose was being cut up. White Fang had gotten a hoof and part of the shinbone, with quite a bit of meat attached. He had taken it off into a thicket to eat it, out of the scramble of other dogs. He was devouring it when Baseek rushed in on him. Before White Fang knew what he was doing, he had slashed Baseek twice and sprung away. His daring and speed surprised the intruder, who stood there gazing stupidly at him.

Baseek was old, and already he had experienced the increasing bravery of the dogs he had bullied. Once he would have sprung upon White Fang in a fury, but he was too old for that now. He bristled fiercely and looked ominously across the shinbone at White Fang. And White Fang, feeling again the old awe, seemed to shrink. He prepared for a graceful retreat.

Here Baseek made his mistake. If he had contented himself with looking fierce and ominous, all would have been well. White Fang would have retreated, leaving the meat to him. But Baseek did not wait. He considered the victory already his and advanced to the meat. As Baseek bent to smell it, White Fang bristled slightly. Even then it was not too late. But the fresh meat was strong in Baseek's nostrils, and greed got the better of him. He took a bite.

This was too much for White Fang. His months of mastery over his teammates made it impossible for him to stand by idly while someone else devoured his meat. As usual, he struck without warning, and his first slash tore Baseek's right ear into ribbons. Baseek was shocked by the suddenness of the whole attack. He was knocked over, his throat was bitten, and while he was getting up, the young dog bit him twice on the shoulder. He made a futile rush at White Fang, missing him with an outraged snap. The next moment Baseek's nose was laid open, and he was staggering backward away from the meat.

The situation was now reversed. White Fang stood over the shin-bone, bristling and menacing, while Baseek stood a little way off, preparing to retreat. He dared not risk a fight with this young lightning-flash, and again he felt the bitter weakness of aging. With dignified calm he turned his back upon the young dog and shin-bone, as though both were unworthy of his notice, and stalked grandly away. Not until well out of sight did he stop to lick his bleeding wounds.

This increased White Fang's pride and

self-confidence. He walked less softly among the grown dogs. Not that he went out of his way looking for trouble—far from it. But he did require respect, demanded to be left alone, and refused to get out of other dogs' way. He could no longer be ignored, as puppies were in general, and as his teammates still were. His teammates had to get out of the way of grown dogs, and had their meat stolen from them. But his puzzled elders accepted White Fang, solitary and cold and dangerous, as an equal. They quickly learned to leave him alone, offering him neither friendliness nor hostility. And he left them alone. After a few encounters with him, they, too, liked it that way.

One day in midsummer, White Fang was investigating a new tepee when he came upon Kiche. He paused and looked at her, remembering her vaguely at first, and then remembering her. That was more than could be said for Kiche, who snarled in menacingly. White Fang's forgotten cubhood, all associated with that familiar snarl, came back to him. She had once been the center of his world. He bounded joyously toward her, and she met him with sharp fangs that laid his cheek open to the bone. Puzzled, he backed away.

But it was not Kiche's fault. A wolf-mother does not remember her cubs of a year or so before, so she did not remember White Fang. She had another litter of puppies now. He was a strange animal, an intruder to be resented.

One of the puppies—his half-brother, though neither knew it—sprawled up to White Fang. He sniffed the puppy curiously, upon which Kiche rushed upon him, gashing his face a second time. He backed farther away. All the old memories died down again and passed into the grave from which they had briefly risen. He looked at Kiche, who was licking her puppy and stopping now and then to snarl at him. He no longer needed her. Neither had any place in the other's world any more.

He was still standing, stupid and bewildered, the memories forgotten, when Kiche attacked him a third time, intent on driving him completely away. White Fang allowed this, for she was a female, and it was the law of their kind that the males must not fight the females. He had not learned this by observing or thinking, but knew it by instinct, in the same way that he feared death and the unknown.

The months went by. White Fang grew stronger, heavier, and more compact, while his character was developing along the lines of his ancestry and his environment. His heritage was like clay, able to be shaped by his environment into many different forms. Had he never come to the man's fire, the Wild would have molded him into a true wolf. But the experience of the gods had made him into a dog—although still a wolfish dog. He took shape according to his surroundings. It made him grouchier, less friendly, and more ferocious. The other dogs increasingly learned to keep the peace with him, and Gray Beaver was coming to value him more greatly.

White Fang seemed very strong in every way, but he had one severe weakness—he could not stand being laughed at. Men might laugh at anything else, but if they laughed at him, he flew into a terrible rage. He lost all control and dignity, behaving like a demon—and woe to the dog who annoyed him at such a time. He knew the law too well to take his anger out on Gray Beaver, a god backed by a club. But the dogs were backed by nothing, and when White Fang came on the scene in such a state, they vanished.

In the third year of his life, a great famine struck the Mackenzie River Indians. In the summer the fish failed. In the winter the caribou did not come. Moose were scarce, the rabbits almost disappeared, and hunting animals perished. Denied their usual food supply and weakened by hunger, predators fell upon and devoured one another. Only the strong survived. White Fang's man-gods were always hunters. The old and the weak died of hunger. The women and children of the village starved so that what little they had might go into the bellies of the lean and hollow-eyed hunters, desperate to bring back meat.

The gods were so desperate that they ate the soft-tanned leather of their moccasins and mittens, while the dogs ate the harnesses off their backs and even the whips. Also, the dogs ate one another, and the gods ate the dogs, weakest first. The dogs that still lived, understood. A few of the boldest and wisest left the fires of the gods, which had now become a shambles, and fled into the forest. There they ultimately starved to death or were eaten by wolves.

In this miserable time, White Fang, too, ran away into the woods. More than the other dogs, he was prepared for this by his cubhood training. He was especially good at stalking small living things, like squirrels, by lying in wait with a patience as great as his hunger. However, there were not enough squirrels, so he hunted even smaller things, like mice. He did not fear fighting a weasel, who was just as hungry and much more ferocious. In the worst times of the famine, he lurked near the fires of the gods, robbing snares and hiding in the forest. He even robbed Gray Beaver's snare of a rabbit at a time when Gray Beaver staggered through the forest, weak and short of breath.

One day White Fang encountered a young wolf, scrawny with famine. If he had not been hungry himself, White Fang might have eventually found his way into the pack among his wild brothers. As it was, he ran the young wolf down, and killed and ate him.

He was fortunate. Always, when hungriest, he found something to kill. When he was weak, none of the larger predators happened to find him. One day a hungry wolf-pack came upon him, but he was strong from two days of eating a lynx. It was a long, cruel chase, but he was better nourished than they, and outran them. Circling back, he even managed to bring down one of his exhausted pursuers.

After that, he journeyed over to the valley where he had been born. Here, in the old lair, he met Kiche. She, too, had fled the gods and returned to her old den to have her puppies. Only one remained alive when White Fang came upon the scene, and this one would soon die of hunger.

Kiche's greeting of her grown son was cold, but he did not mind. He had outgrown his mother. So he left and trotted on up the stream. At the forks he turned left, where he found the abandoned lair of the lynx with whom his mother and he had fought long before. Here he settled down and rested for a day.

During the early summer, in the last days of the famine, he met Lip-lip. He, too, had taken to the woods, barely surviving. White Fang came upon him unexpectedly. Trotting in opposite directions along the base of a high cliff, they rounded a corner and found themselves face to face. They measured each other with suspicion and alarm.

White Fang was in splendid condition. For the past week he had eaten his fill, and was even gorged from his latest kill. But the moment he looked at Lip-lip, his hair rose all along his back, and he snarled. It was a reflex, the same reaction that had always been produced by Lip-lip's bullying. Lip-lip tried to back off, but White Fang wasted no time, striking him hard, shoulder to shoulder. Lip-lip was thrown on his back, and White Fang's teeth drove into the scrawny throat. Lip-lip was mortally wounded. As he struggled vainly for life, White Fang walked around, stiff-legged and observant. When Lip-lip expired, he resumed his trot along the base of the bluff.

One day, not long thereafter, he came to the edge of the forest, where a narrow stretch of open land sloped down to the Mackenzie.

When he had been over this ground before, it had been bare, but now it had a village. Still hidden in the trees, he paused to study the situation. Sights and sounds and scents were familiar. It was the old village changed to a new place. The sights and sounds and smells were familiar, but different from the way he remembered. There was neither whimpering nor wailing. He heard a woman's angry voice, and knew it to be the anger of a full stomach. He smelled fish. The famine was over. He came out boldly from the forest and trotted into camp, straight to Gray Beaver's tepee. Gray Beaver was not there, but Kloo-kooch welcomed him with glad cries and a whole fresh-caught fish, and he lay down to await Gray Beaver.

PART FOUR:
THE SUPERIOR GODS

CHAPTER ONE
THE ENEMY OF HIS KIND

If there had ever been any chance that White Fang might become friends with his own kind, it was destroyed forever when he was made leader of the sled-team. For now the dogs hated him—hated him for the extra meat Mit-sah gave him, and for the real and imagined special favors he received. They hated that he was at the head of the team; his brushlike tail and retreating hindquarters constantly drove the other dogs crazy. And White Fang hated them back. He also hated being sled-leader, because it meant that he had to run away in front of the pack. For three years, he had beaten every one of them up, dominating them. However, he must endure this job or die, and he was not ready to die.

The moment Mit-sah commanded them to move, the whole team sprang forward at White Fang with eager, savage cries. There was no escape for him. If he turned upon them, Mit-sah would lash him in the face with the stinging whip. His tail and hindquarters were hardly useful weapons against so many merciless fangs. There was nothing for him to do but run away, offending his own nature and pride with every leap he made. This offense, enforced by the will of the gods and the caribou-gut whip, doubled the bitterness in his heart. His hatred grew as great as the ferocity and determination of his nature.

If ever a creature was the enemy of its kind, it was White Fang. He asked for no mercy and gave none. He continually traded scars with the pack. Unlike most team leaders, when he was out of harness in camp, he did not huddle near the gods for protection. He walked about boldly, inflicting punishment in the night for what he had suffered in the day. In the past, they had learned to avoid him, but now it was different. All day their eyes saw him seeming to run away from them, so they did not feel they had to yield to him now. When he came among them, there was always a squabble of snarls and snaps and growls. It was as though he breathed in hatred and malice from the very air.

When Mit-sah ordered the team to stop, White Fang obeyed. At first, these halts caused trouble with the other dogs. All of them would spring upon the hated leader, only to find the tables turned. Behind him was Mit-sah, the great whip singing in his hand. So the dogs came to understand that when the team stopped on orders, White Fang was to be let alone. But if White Fang stopped without orders, they were allowed to attack and destroy him if they could. Soon, White Fang no longer stopped without orders. He learned quickly, as he must to survive in such unusually severe conditions.

But the dogs could never learn to leave him alone in camp. Each day's work of pursuing him erased the lesson they had learned in camp the night before, so they would have to relearn and forget it over and over again. They did not, however, forget that he seemed different from them, which was enough reason by itself for them to be hostile. Like him, they were domesticated wolves, but they were several generations removed from the Wild. To them, it was an unknown, terrible, menacing place. And White Fang symbolized it. When they showed him their teeth, they were defending themselves from the unknown powers of destruction that lurked in the shadows of the forest and in the dark beyond the campfire.

But there was one lesson the dogs did

learn—to keep together. None of them could face White Fang alone. If they had come at him one at a time, he would have killed them all, one by one, in a single night. As it was, he never had a chance to kill them. He might roll a dog off its feet, but the pack would be upon him before he could follow up and deliver the deadly throat-stroke. At the first hint of conflict, the whole team drew together and faced him. The dogs quarreled among themselves, but when trouble was brewing with White Fang, they forgot their squabbles.

On the other hand, try as they might, they could not kill White Fang. He was too quick, tough and wise. He avoided tight places and always escaped when the others looked likely to surround him. No dog among them could get him off his feet, which he kept under him as surely as he clung to life. In this unending warfare, life and footing were the same thing, and none knew that better than White Fang.

So he became the enemy of his kind, of those domesticated wolves who were softened by the fires of man and weakened from living in the sheltering shadow of man's strength. White Fang was molded into a bitter, merciless creature. He declared a fierce, eternal vengeance against all dogs, one so savage that even Gray Beaver—who was quite fierce in his own right—had to marvel at White Fang's ferocity. He swore that there had never before been an animal like White Fang. When the Indians in strange villages considered his killings among their own dogs, they agreed.

When White Fang was nearly five years old, Gray Beaver took him on another great journey down the Mackenzie, across the Rockies, and down to the Yukon River. The many villages along the way would long remember the havoc he created among their dogs. He loved taking vengeance on his own kind. They were ordinary, unsuspecting dogs, unprepared for his sudden, direct attack. He was a lightning-flash of slaughter. While they were wasting time bristling and challenging him stiff-legged, he was snapping into action like a steel spring. Before they knew what was happening, he had their throats open.

He became a great, efficient fighter. He never wasted his strength, never wrestled. He leaped in too quickly for that, and, if he missed, was out again too quickly. Wolves do not like being cooped up with other creatures, and White Fang disliked it to an extreme. He could not endure prolonged contact with another body. It felt like danger and made him frantic. He must be away, free, on his own legs and touching no living thing. This was the Wild within him. In contact there lurked danger, a trap waiting to take his life.

So, the strange dogs he encountered had no chance against him. He either hurt or killed them, or got away untouched. There were, of course, occasional exceptions. A few times, several dogs jumped him at once and punished him before he could get away. In a few other instances, single dogs cut deeply into him. But these were accidents. He fought so effectively that he normally came out unhurt.

Another advantage he had was being able to judge time and distance correctly, much better than the average dog, and without having to think. His eyes saw an action, and his brain knew the limits of that action and the amount of time it would take. Thus, he could avoid the leap of another dog, or the drive of its fangs, and at the same time could choose the exact instant in which to counterattack. Nature had gifted his mind and body with perfect timing.

In the summer, White Fang arrived at Fort Yukon. Gray Beaver had crossed the great divide between Mackenzie and the Yukon in the late winter, and spent the spring hunting among the outlying western spurs of the Rockies. After the ice broke up, he had built a canoe and paddled down the Porcupine River to where it emptied into the Yukon, just south of the Arctic Circle.

The old Hudson's Bay Company fort stood here, with many Indians, much food, and excitement of a sort never seen before. It was the gold rush summer of 1898, and thousands of gold-hunters were going up the Yukon to Dawson City and the Klondike. Many had been traveling for over a year, but were still hundreds of miles from their goal. All had traveled at least five thousand miles, and some had come from the other side of the world.

Gray Beaver stopped at the fort. He had heard rumors of the gold rush, and he had brought many furs, mittens and moccasins to sell, expecting good profit. As it turned out, the profit was ten times greater than he had imagined in his wildest dreams. Like most of his people, he traded carefully and slowly, willing to take all summer and the rest of the winter to sell all his products.

At Fort Yukon, White Fang saw his first white men. Although the tepees of the Indians had impressed him, he was even more impressed now by the houses and the huge fort of massive logs. The larger something loomed over him, the more power he associated with its owners. Thus, he sensed that the white men were a race of superior gods, with greater mastery over things than the gods he had known until now. Gray Beaver seemed like a child-god in comparison.

As a result, White Fang was suspicious of the white men. If they were superior gods, who knew what unknown terrors and hurts they could inflict? For the first few hours, he watched them carefully, from a distance, avoiding notice. When he saw that no harm came to dogs that approached them, he came closer. The men were very curious about his wolfish appearance, and pointed him out to one another. This act put White Fang on his guard, so that when they tried to approach him, he showed his teeth and backed away. Fortunately for them, none succeeded in laying a hand on him.

White Fang soon learned that only a dozen of these gods lived here. Every two or three days a steamship—another colossal display of power—stopped off for several hours. The white men got off these steamers and went away on them again. There seemed to be untold numbers of these white men. In the first day or so, he saw more of them than he had seen Indians in all his life, and they continued to come and go.

But if the white gods were all-powerful, their dogs did not amount to much. This White Fang quickly discovered from his meetings with those brought ashore with their masters. They were all different shapes and sizes. Some were too short-legged; others too long-legged. They had hair instead of fur, and a few had very little hair. And none of them knew how to fight.

The white gods' dogs were the enemies of White Fang's kind, so he was inclined to fight them. He quickly learned to scorn them deeply. They were soft and helpless, made much noise, and floundered around clumsily, trying to accomplish by raw strength what he achieved through dexterity and cunning. They would bellow and rush at him; he sprang to the side. While they wondered where he was, he struck them on the shoulder, knocked them off their feet, and went for their throats.

Sometimes this stroke scored, and a wounded dog rolled in the dirt, to be pounced upon and torn to pieces by the waiting pack of Indian dogs. White Fang was very wise. He had long since learned that the gods—including white ones—got angry when their dogs were killed. So when he had slashed open the dog's throat, he dropped back and let the pack finish it off. It was then that the white men rushed in, taking their anger out on the pack with stones, clubs, axes and other weapons, while White Fang was content to stand at a distance and watch them get hurt.

But his fellows also learned, and White Fang learned with them. They learned that it was when a steamer first tied up to the bank that they had their fun. After the first two or three strange dogs had been destroyed, the white men hustled their own animals back on board and took savage vengeance on the offenders. One white man, having seen his dog torn to pieces before his eyes, drew a revolver and fired rapidly. Soon six of the pack lay dead or dying—another show of power that sank deep into White Fang's mind.

White Fang enjoyed it all. He did not love his kind, and he was smart enough to escape hurt himself. At first, the killing of the white men's dogs had been a hobby. Since he didn't have any work to do, it became his job. Gray Beaver was busy trading and getting wealthy. So White Fang hung around the landing with the notorious gang of Indian dogs, waiting for steamers. The fun began when one of the boats arrived. After a few minutes of chaos, before the white men had gotten over their surprise, the gang scattered. The fun was over

until the next steamer showed up.

He was not, however, a member of the gang. He remained apart from it and was feared by it. He picked the fights, but left the gang to take the consequences. The fights were easily picked. All he had to do was show himself and trigger the strange dogs' irresistible instinct to attack and destroy him. He was the Wild— unknown, terrible, always menacing. He was the thing their ancestors had deserted when they came in to the fires. For centuries, their masters had encouraged them to protect themselves and their gods by killing things of the Wild. Therefore, fresh from the soft southern world, the town-reared dogs' instinctive fear of the Wild drove them to continue the ancient battle.

All of this made White Fang's days enjoyable. If the sight of him brought these strange dogs down upon him, so much the better for him, and so much the worse for them. Each saw the other as fair game.

White Fang's whole experience had shaped him. He had first seen the light of day in a lonely lair. His first fights had been with the grouse, the weasel and the lynx. His whole puppyhood had been made bitter by the cruelty of Lip-lip and the puppy pack. If not for Lip-lip, he would have grown up together with the puppies and developed more liking for dogs. If Gray Beaver had shown him affection and love, it might have brought out all kinds of kindly qualities. These things had not been so. The clay of White Fang had been molded until he became what he was, gloomy and lonely, unloving and ferocious, the enemy of all his kind.

CHAPTER TWO
THE MAD GOD

A small number of white men lived in Fort Yukon. These men had been in the country a long time, and took great pride in calling themselves "sourdoughs." They were called this because, lacking baking powder, they made their bread from sourdough. Scornfully, they called the new men from the steamers "cheechakos"—that is, "tenderfeet"—a title the new men did not like. Sourdoughs liked watching cheechakos get into trouble, and they especially enjoyed the havoc White Fang and his gang caused among the newcomers' dogs. When a steamer arrived, the men of the fort hurried down to the bank to watch the fun. They looked forward to it as much as the Indian dogs did, and they noticed the savage and crafty part that White Fang played.

But there was one man among them who enjoyed the sport most. He would come running at the first sound of a steamboat's whistle, and when the last fight was over and the dogs had scattered, he would return slowly to the fort, his face heavy with regret. Sometimes, when a soft Southland dog went down, shrieking its death-cry under the fangs of the pack, this man got so excited he leaped into the air, cheering with delight. He watched and wanted White Fang most of all.

This man was called "Beauty." No one knew his first name, and he was known in the country as Beauty Smith. But he was no beauty. A small man, he had an abnormally small, pointed head. In fact, as a boy, he had been called "Pinhead." He had a low, wide forehead, and big, muddy, yellow eyes that were too far apart in a wide face. His hair and beard were scraggly, dirty-yellow clumps like tufts of grain.

He also had a lower jaw so huge that it seemed to rest on his chest, with two big, yellow teeth sticking out like fangs at each side. His slender neck made the jaw look even bigger, which made him look ferocious and determined. But this was a lie. Beauty Smith was known far and wide as a weak-kneed and sniveling coward.

In short, Beauty Smith was a monstrosity, and it wasn't his fault. He did the cooking, dishwashing and other basic work for the men in the fort. They tolerated him, as people tolerate those who were born with hard luck. They also feared him. His cowardly rages made them afraid he would shoot them in the back or poison their coffee. But somebody had to do the cooking, and whatever his other shortcomings, Beauty Smith could cook.

This was the man that delighted in White Fang's ferocity and wanted to own him. He tried to entice White Fang from the beginning, but was ignored. When Beauty Smith became more insistent, White Fang bristled, bared his teeth, and backed away. He sensed the deep, unhealthy evil in the man, and feared the extended hand and the attempts at soft-spoken speech. White Fang's understanding of evil was of something likely to give hurt, and he hated Beauty Smith accordingly.

White Fang was in Gray Beaver's camp when Beauty Smith first visited it. At the faint sound of his footsteps, White Fang knew who was coming and began to bristle. He had been lying down in comfort, but he arose quickly, and, as the man arrived, slid away wolflike to the edge of the camp. He could see the man and Gray Beaver talking together. Once, the man pointed at him, and White Fang snarled back as though the hand were much nearer. Beauty Smith laughed at this, and White Fang slunk away to the sheltering woods, keeping a careful eye on him.

Gray Beaver refused to sell the dog. He had grown rich from trading and needed nothing, he said. Besides, White Fang was a valuable animal, the strongest sled-dog he had ever owned, and the best leader. Furthermore, there was no dog like him on the Mackenzie or the Yukon. He killed other dogs as easily as men killed mosquitoes, said Gray Beaver, making Beauty Smith's eyes light up eagerly. No, stated the Indian, White Fang was not for sale at any price.

But Beauty Smith knew the ways of Indians. He visited Gray Beaver's camp often, and hidden under his coat was always a black bottle of whisky, which makes men thirst for more of it. Gray Beaver wanted more of the liquid, and his alcohol-hazed brain was willing to do anything to get it. He began to go through the money he had received for his furs and mittens, and as he did, his temper grew shorter. Eventually he was out of money and tremendously thirsty. It was then that Beauty Smith came to talk to him about selling White Fang. But this time the price offered was in bottles, not dollars, and Gray Beaver's ears perked up.

"You ketch dog, you take him all right," was his last word.

The bottles were delivered, but after two days of useless efforts to catch White Fang, Beauty Smith came to Gray Beaver and said, "You ketch dog."

White Fang slunk into camp one evening

and dropped down with a sigh of contentment. The dreaded white god was not there. For days he had been trying to catch him, compelling White Fang to avoid the camp. He did not know what evil those hands threatened, but he knew that he had best keep away from them.

But he had just lain down when Gray Beaver staggered over to him and tied a leather thong around his neck. He sat down beside White Fang, holding the end of the thong in his hand, drinking deeply. An hour passed, and White Fang recognized the feel of a certain pair of approaching footsteps. He bristled in recognition and tried to draw the thong out of Gray Beaver's hands, but the fingers closed tightly as the Indian got up.

Beauty Smith strode into camp and stood over White Fang. He snarled softly up at the evil creature, watching the hands keenly. One began to descend toward his head. His soft snarl grew tense and harsh. The hand continued downward as his snarls shortened. Suddenly he snapped, striking with his fangs like a snake. The hand was jerked back, and the teeth came together emptily with a sharp click. Beauty Smith was frightened and angry. Gray Beaver smacked White Fang alongside the head, so that he cowered down close to the earth in respectful obedience.

White Fang's suspicious eyes followed every movement. He saw Beauty Smith go away and return with a stout club. Then Gray Beaver gave him the thong, and Beauty Smith started to walk away. The thong grew tight, and White Fang resisted. Gray Beaver hit him to get him moving. He obeyed—in a way—by hurling himself upon the stranger who was dragging him away. Beauty Smith did not jump away. He had been waiting for this. He swung the club smartly, stopping the rush midway and smashing White Fang to the ground. Gray Beaver laughed and nodded approval. Beauty Smith tightened the thong again, and White Fang crawled limply and dizzily to his feet.

He did not rush a second time. One smash from the club was sufficient to convince him that the white god knew how to handle it, and he was too wise to fight when he couldn't win. So he followed unhappily at Beauty Smith's heels, his tail between his legs, yet snarling softly under his breath. But the white man kept a wary eye on him, and the club was held always ready to strike.

At the fort, Beauty Smith left him securely tied and went in to bed. White Fang waited an hour, then put his teeth to the thong and was free in ten seconds. There had been no useless gnawing. The thong was cut almost as cleanly as though done by a knife. White Fang looked up at the fort, at the same time bristling and growling. Then he turned and trotted back to Gray Beaver's camp. He owed no loyalty to this strange and terrible god. He had given himself to Gray Beaver, and in his mind nothing had changed.

But what had occurred once before was repeated—with a difference. Gray Beaver again tied him with a thong, and in the morning turned him over to Beauty Smith, who began to beat him. White Fang, tied securely, could only rage in vain and endure the punishment. With the club and the whip, he gave White Fang a beating that made the first one given in his puppyhood by Gray Beaver seem mild.

The difference was that Beauty Smith enjoyed beating his victim, gloating with a dull flame in his eyes as he swung the weapons and listened to White Fang's helpless cries and snarls. Like most cowards, Beauty Smith was cruel. He would cringe and snivel before the blows or angry words of a man, but he would take his revenge upon weaker creatures. He had come into the world malformed, and life had twisted his mind to match.

White Fang knew why he was being beaten. When Gray Beaver tied the thong around his neck, and gave it to Beauty Smith, White Fang knew that it was his god's will for him to go with Beauty Smith. And when Beauty Smith left him tied outside the fort, he knew that it was Beauty Smith's will that he should remain there. Therefore, his disobedience of the gods had earned punishment. He had seen dogs change owners in the past, and he had seen the runaways beaten as he was being beaten. He was wise, but there were other forces in his nature, such as loyalty. He did not love Gray Beaver, but the deep loyalty within him—so typical of and unique to dogs—kept him faithful to the man.

After the beating, White Fang was dragged back to the fort. But this time Beauty Smith left him tied with a stick.

One does not give up a god easily, nor did White Fang. Gray Beaver was his own particular god, and despite Gray Beaver's will, White Fang would not give him up. Gray Beaver's betrayal had no effect upon him. He had surrendered body and soul without reservation, and this had created a very strong bond.

So, when the men in the fort were asleep, White Fang got to work on the stick that held him. The wood was seasoned and dry, and it

was tied so closely to his neck that it took him a great deal of patient effort to get his teeth onto it. After many hours of hard work, he succeeded in gnawing through it. This was something that dogs normally never did. But White Fang did it, trotting away from the fort in the early morning with the end of the stick hanging from his neck.

He was wise, but more faithful than wise, or else he would not have gone back to Gray Beaver, who had already twice betrayed him. He went back to be betrayed yet a third time. Again he yielded to Gray Beaver's thong around his neck, and again Beauty Smith came to claim him. And this time he was beaten even more severely than before.

Gray Beaver looked on without emotion while the white man used the whip. It was no longer his dog. When the beating was over, White Fang was in bad shape. A soft, Southland dog would have died, but not he. His experiences had made him too tough, and he clutched life too strongly, but he was badly hurt. At first he was unable to drag himself along, and Beauty Smith had to wait half an hour for him. Finally, blind and staggering, he followed Beauty Smith back to the fort.

But now he was tied with a chain that defied his teeth, and he lunged in vain in an effort to pull the steel fastener from the timber into which it was driven. After a few days, sober and bankrupt, Gray Beaver departed up the Porcupine River on his long journey to the Mackenzie. White Fang remained on the Yukon, the property of a terrible, mad god. White Fang knew nothing of madness; he knew only that he must submit to this new master's every whim and fancy.

CHAPTER THREE
THE REIGN OF HATE

Under the treatment of the mad god, White Fang became a fiend. He was kept chained in a pen at the rear of the fort, and here Beauty Smith teased and drove him wild with petty torments. He discovered early on how much White Fang disliked being laughed at, so any time he played a painful trick on White Fang, he laughed and pointed at him. This drove him into rages so terrible that he had even less sense and more madness than Beauty Smith.

Before now, White Fang had been merely the ferocious enemy of his own kind. He now became the enemy of all things, and more ferocious than ever. He was so tortured that he hated blindly and without any spark of reason. He hated the chain that bound him, the men who peered in at him through the slats of the pen, and their dogs that snarled evilly at him in his helplessness. He hated the very wood of the pen that confined him. And, above all, he hated Beauty Smith.

But Beauty Smith's cruelties had a purpose. One day a number of men gathered about the pen. Beauty Smith entered, club in hand, and took the chain off White Fang's neck. When his master had gone out, White Fang tore around the pen, trying to get at the men outside. He was impressive and terrible. Fully five feet long, and standing two and one-half feet tall at the shoulder, he far outweighed a wolf of normal size. He had inherited the heavier build of the dog from his mother, so that he weighed over ninety pounds. It was all muscle and bone, not an ounce of fat. He was a fighting creature in the finest condition.

The door of the pen was being opened again. White Fang paused. Something unusual was happening. He waited. The door was opened wider. Then a huge dog was thrust inside, and the door was slammed shut behind him. White Fang had never seen such a dog. It was a mastiff, an enormous breed with very powerful jaws, but its size and fierce appearance did not make him think twice. Here was something besides wood and iron that he could vent his hatred on. He leaped in with a flash of fangs that ripped down the side of the mastiff's neck. The mastiff shook his head, growled hoarsely, and plunged at White Fang. But White Fang was here, there, and everywhere, always evading and eluding, and always leaping in and slashing with his fangs and leaping out again in time to escape punishment.

The men outside shouted and applauded, while Beauty Smith gloated in thrilled delight over the ripping and mangling White Fang inflicted. There had never been any hope for the mastiff; he was too awkward and slow. In the end, Beauty Smith beat White Fang back with a club so that the mastiff's owner could drag it out. Bets were paid, and money clinked in Beauty Smith's hand.

White Fang came to look forward eagerly to the gathering of the men around his pen. It meant a fight, and this was the only way that he now had to express his life. Tormented, driven to hate, he was kept a prisoner so that there was no way to satisfy that hate except when his master pitted another dog against him. Beauty Smith had been a good judge of talent, for White Fang always won. One day, three dogs were turned in upon him, one after the other. Another day a full-grown wolf, freshly caught from the Wild, was shoved in through the door of the pen. And on still another day, two dogs were set against him at the same time. This was his toughest fight, and in the end he killed them both—though they half killed him.

In the fall of the year, when the first snows were falling and slushy ice chunks were running in the river, Beauty Smith took White

Fang on a steamboat trip up the Yukon to Dawson. White Fang had now achieved a reputation in the land as the "Fighting Wolf," and curious men usually surrounded his cage on the steamer's deck. He raged and snarled at them, or lay quietly and studied them with cold hatred. This hate was his life, his hell, his only passion. His kind were not designed to be cooped up like this. Men stared at him, poked sticks at him to make him snarl, and then laughed at him.

In so doing, these men were molding him into something more ferocious than Nature had intended. Nevertheless, Nature had made him adaptable. Where many another animal would have died or had its spirit broken, he adjusted himself and lived, with no loss of spirit. Beauty Smith, arch-fiend and tormentor, might have been capable of breaking White Fang's spirit, but there were no signs that he was succeeding.

If Beauty Smith had a devil in him, so did White Fang, and the two of them raged endlessly against each other. Before, White Fang had enough sense to cower down before a man with a club in his hand, but not anymore. The mere sight of Beauty Smith was enough to send him into a wild fury. And when they came close together, and he had been beaten back by the club, he remained defiant. No matter how terribly he was beaten, he continued to growl. And when Beauty Smith gave up and withdrew, White Fang growled defiance at his retreating back, or sprang at the bars of the cage, bellowing his hatred.

When the steamboat arrived at Dawson, White Fang went ashore. But he still lived a public life, in a cage surrounded by curious men. He was shown off as the "Fighting Wolf," and men paid fifty cents in gold dust to see him.

He was given no rest. If he lay down to sleep, he was poked with a sharp stick. This kept him in a rage most of the time, making sure that the audience got its money's worth. But worst of all was the effect of this situation on his mind. The men regarded him as the most fearful of wild beasts, and their every word and action reminded him of his own deadliness. His ferocity fed on itself and increased.

In addition to being exhibited, he was a professional fighting animal. Whenever a fight could be arranged, he was taken out of his cage and led off into the woods a few miles from town. Usually this occurred at night, so as to avoid trouble with the Northwest Mounted Police, who kept order in the

Territory. After a few hours of waiting, the audience and the challenger arrived. White Fang eventually fought many sizes and breeds of dogs. It was a savage land full of savage men, and the fights were usually to the death.

White Fang continued to fight, while the other dogs died. He never lost. His early training, fighting Lip-lip and the whole puppy-pack, paid off now. No dog could push him over. This was the favorite trick of the wolf breeds—to rush in upon an enemy, either directly or with an unexpected swerve, strike his shoulder, and knock him off his feet. Mackenzie hounds, Eskimo and Labrador dogs, huskies and Malamutes—all tried and failed. Men spoke of this, and waited for the day he would be knocked over, but White Fang always disappointed them.

Then there was his lightning quickness. It gave him a tremendous advantage over his enemies. No matter how experienced they were, they had never fought a dog that moved so swiftly. The suddenness of his attack also gave him another great advantage. The average dog was used to the ritual of snarling and bristling and growling before the fight. But since White Fang never bothered with this, the dog was knocked off his feet and finished before he had begun to fight. This happened

so often that the men made a practice of holding White Fang until the other dog went through the whole ritual and got around to making the first attack.

But the greatest advantage White Fang had was his experience. He knew more about fighting than any of the dogs that faced him. He had fought more fights, knew how to defeat more tricks and methods, and had more tricks himself. His own technique could not be improved upon.

As time went by, he had fewer and fewer fights. Finding him an equal match was impossible, and Beauty Smith had to pit him against wolves, which were trapped by the Indians for the purpose. A fight between White Fang and a wolf always drew a crowd. Once, a full-grown female lynx was brought, and this time White Fang fought for his life.

She was as quick and ferocious as he, and fought with her sharp-clawed feet while he fought with his fangs alone.

But after the lynx, White Fang fought no more. There were no more animals considered worthy of fighting with him. So he remained on display until spring, when a card dealer named Tim Keenan arrived, bringing the first bulldog to the Klondike. The fight was inevitable, and for a week it was the main subject of discussion in certain parts of town.

CHAPTER FOUR
THE CLINGING DEATH

Beauty Smith slipped the chain from White Fang's neck and stepped back.

For once, White Fang did not attack immediately. He stood still, ears forward, alertly examining the strange animal. He had never seen such a dog before. Tim Keenan muttered, "Go to it," shoving the bulldog forward. The short, clumsy-looking animal waddled toward the center of the circle. He stopped and blinked across at White Fang.

The crowd cried, "Go to him, Cherokee! Sick 'm, Cherokee! Eat 'm up!"

But Cherokee, the bulldog, did not seem anxious to fight. He turned his head and blinked at the men who shouted, wagging his stumpy tail. He was not afraid, just lazy. Besides, this wasn't the kind of dog he usually fought. He was waiting for them to bring the real dog.

Tim Keenan stepped in and bent over Cherokee, rubbing his fur the wrong way, pushing him slightly toward White Fang. Cherokee became irritated and began to growl softly, deep down in his throat.

This made the hair rise on White Fang's neck and shoulders. Tim Keenan gave a final shove and stepped back again. Cherokee continued forward on his own, bowlegged but swift.

Then White Fang struck. A cry of startled admiration went up. He had leaped in like a cat, slashed with his fangs, and then leaped clear. The bulldog was bleeding from a rip in the back of his thick neck. He did not even snarl, but turned and followed White Fang.

The display on both sides, the quickness of one against the steadiness of the other, had gotten the crowd excited. Old bets were being increased; new bets were made. Again and again, White Fang sprang in, slashed, and got away untouched. Still his strange foe followed him, businesslike. There was a purpose to his method, and he refused to be distracted from his job.

His whole behavior was based upon this purpose. It puzzled White Fang. He had never seen such a dog. Its skin was easily broken. There was no thick mat of fur to repel White Fang's teeth, such as his own breed had. His teeth drew blood easily on every strike, while the enemy seemed defenseless. Also, unlike the other dogs he had fought, it did not cry out. Except for growls and grunts, the dog took its punishment silently and kept pursuing him.

Cherokee could turn and whirl swiftly enough, but White Fang was never there. Cherokee, too, was puzzled. He had never fought a dog he could not draw in closely to fight. Most dogs readily drew close. But here was a dog that kept his distance, dancing and dodging here and there. And when it did get its teeth into him, it let go instantly and darted away.

But White Fang could not get at the soft underside of the throat. The bulldog stood too short, and its massive jaws gave extra protection. White Fang darted in and out unhurt, while Cherokee's wounds increased. Both sides of his neck and head were ripped and slashed. He bled freely, but continued his plodding pursuit. Once, he was so baffled he came to a full stop and blinked at the watching men, at the same time wagging his stump of a tail to show his willingness to fight.

In that moment White Fang darted in and out, ripping his trimmed remnant of an ear. With a slight display of anger, Cherokee took up the pursuit again, running on the inside of the circle White Fang was making, and trying to fasten his deadly grip on White Fang's throat. The bulldog missed by a hair, and men cried out praise as White Fang zipped out of danger in the opposite direction.

The time went by. White Fang danced on, dodging and leaping in and out, always doing damage. And still the bulldog, grim and certain, toiled after him. Sooner or later he would get the grip that meant victory. In the meantime, he accepted all the punishment he got. His ears, neck, shoulders, and even his lips were cut and bleeding—all from these lightning snaps he could not prevent. Time and again White Fang had attempted to knock Cherokee over, but Cherokee was too close to the ground.

White Fang tried the trick once too often. He caught Cherokee with his head turned away, shoulder exposed, and crashed in. But his own shoulder was high above the bulldog, and he struck so hard that he continued on over the other's body. For the first time in his fighting history, White Fang lost his footing. His body turned a half-somersault in the air, and he would have landed on his back had he not twisted in the air, catlike, fall feet first to the earth. As it was, he landed heavily on his side. The next instant he was on his feet, but in that instant Cherokee's teeth closed on his throat.

It was not a good grip, being too low down toward the chest, but Cherokee held on. White Fang sprang to his feet and tore

wildly around, trying to shake off the bulldog. The clinging, dragging weight hampered his movement and made him frantic. His whole being rebelled madly against the restriction. Movement had always meant continued life, and now he could barely move.

For several minutes, White Fang was basically insane. He whirled, turned, reversed, did everything he could think of to shake the fifty-pound weight hanging from his throat. The bulldog merely kept his grip. Occasionally, he managed to get his feet on the earth and brace himself against White Fang, but the next moment he would lose his footing and be dragged around in the whirl of one of White Fang's mad twists. Cherokee's grip was his identity. Holding on was very satisfying, no matter how much he was hurled around or hurt. Only the grip mattered, and he hung on.

White Fang began to tire. It had never worked out this way, and he did not understand. With all the other dogs he had fought, it had been the same: snap and slash and get away. He lay partly on his side, panting for breath. Cherokee, still holding his grip, tried to get him over entirely on his side. White Fang resisted, and he could feel the jaws shifting their grip, slightly relaxing and closing again in a chewing movement. Each shift brought the grip closer to his throat. The bulldog's method was to hold on, and when White Fang wasn't moving, to improve the grip. When White Fang struggled, Cherokee was content merely to hold on.

The bulging back of Cherokee's neck was the only part of him that White Fang's teeth could reach. He bit near the base of the neck, but he did not know the chewing method of fighting, nor were his jaws suited to it. For a moment, he spasmodically ripped and tore with his fangs. Then the dogs' positions shifted, and the bulldog managed to roll him over on his back and get on top of him, still hanging on to his throat. Again like a cat, White Fang curled his hindquarters in, and with his rear feet, he began to claw his enemy's underbelly with long tearing-strokes. Cherokee might have been gutted had he not quickly moved his body off White Fang's. He kept his grip and landed at an angle to White Fang, safe from the rear claws.

There was no escaping that grip. It shifted slowly up along the jugular. All that saved White Fang from death was the loose skin of his neck and the thick fur that covered it, which filled up Cherokee's mouth. Cherokee's bite could barely penetrate White Fang's skin and fur, but he was gradually pulling more of both into his mouth. This was slowly strangling White Fang, who was beginning to have trouble breathing.

It began to look as though the battle were over. Those who had bet on Cherokee crowed in triumph, and offered ridiculous odds. White Fang's backers were depressed, and refused bets of ten to one and twenty to one, though one man—Beauty Smith—was reckless enough to accept a bet of fifty to one. He then stepped into the ring and pointed his finger at White Fang, and began to laugh scornfully. White Fang went wild with rage. He called up his reserves of strength, and got onto his feet. As he struggled around the ring, fifty pounds of bulldog hanging from his throat, his anger gave way to panic. He reared and struggled frantically in a vain effort to shake off the clinging death.

At last he toppled backward, exhausted. The bulldog promptly shifted his grip, mangling more and more of the fur-folded flesh, choking White Fang more severely. There were many cries of "Cherokee!" "Cherokee!" for the apparent winner. Cherokee responded by wagging his stubby tail, but did not let this shake his terrible grip.

Then something else distracted the spectators. Bells jingled. Dog-mushers' cries were heard. Everybody but Beauty Smith looked worried that it might be the police. But they saw two men running with sled and dogs, evidently coming down the creek from a gold-prospecting trip. At sight of the crowd, they stopped their dogs and came over, curious to see the cause of the excitement. The dog-musher had a mustache, but the other, taller and younger, was clean-shaven, with cheeks that were rosy from the frosty air.

White Fang had nearly ceased struggling. Now and again he made a futile effort to resist, but his air supply was lessening. Had the bulldog's initial grip not been so low down, his throat-vein would have long since been torn open. But the shifting had taken a long time and clogged the heavy jaws with White Fang's fur and folded skin.

In the meantime, the brute in Beauty Smith was rising to the surface. When he saw White Fang's eyes glazing, he knew beyond doubt that the fight was lost. He lost control, sprang upon White Fang, and began to kick him savagely. The crowd hissed and protested, but that was all.

While this went on, and Beauty Smith continued to kick White Fang, there was a commotion in the crowd. The tall young newcomer was forcing his way through, pushing everyone aside. When he broke through into the ring, Beauty Smith was just about to deliver another kick, so he was on one foot. At that moment, the newcomer punched him in the face. Beauty Smith's whole body went airborne as he turned over backward and hit the snow. The newcomer turned upon the crowd.

"You cowards!" he cried. "You beasts!"

He was in a rage himself—a sane rage. His steely gray eyes flashed upon the crowd. Beauty Smith got up and came toward him, sniffling and cowardly. The newcomer did not realize just what a coward the other was, and assumed he was coming back to fight. So, with a "You beast!" he smashed Beauty Smith over backward with a second blow in the face. Beauty Smith decided that the snow was the safest place for him, and so he lay where he fell.

"Come on, Matt, lend a hand," the newcomer called the dog-musher, who had followed him into the ring.

Both men bent over the dogs. Matt took hold of White Fang, ready to pull when Cherokee's jaws were loosened. The younger man clutched the bulldog's jaws in his hands and tried to spread them. As he tugged and wrenched without success, he kept saying, "Beasts!"

The crowd began to grow unruly, and some of the men protested the spoiling of the fun. They shut up when the newcomer lifted his head for a moment and glared at them.

"You damn beasts!" he finally exploded, and went back to his task.

"It's no use, Mr. Scott, you can't break 'em apart that way," Matt said at last.

The pair surveyed the locked dogs. "Ain't bleedin' much," Matt announced. "Ain't got all the way in yet."

"But he's liable to any moment," Scott answered. "There, did you see that? He shifted his grip up a bit."

The younger man grew more worried about White Fang. He struck Cherokee savagely on the head again and again, but the jaws held firm. Cherokee wagged his tail, showing that he understood the meaning of the beating, but knew he was doing his duty by keeping his grip.

"Won't some of you help?" Scott cried desperately at the crowd. But no help was offered, just sarcastic cheers and phony advice.

"You'll have to get a prying tool of some sort," Matt suggested. The other reached into his holster, drew his revolver, and tried to push its barrel between the bulldog's jaws. He shoved hard until the steel grated against the locked teeth.

Tim Keenan strode into the ring. He paused beside Scott and touched him on the shoulder, saying ominously, "Don't break them teeth, stranger."

"Then I'll break his neck," Scott retorted, continuing his shoving and wedging with the revolver muzzle.

"I said, don't break them teeth," the card-dealer repeated, more ominously than before.

If he was bluffing, it didn't work. Scott continued his efforts, though he looked up coolly and asked, "Your dog?"

The card-dealer grunted.

"Then get in here and break this grip."

"Well, stranger," the other drawled irritatingly, "I don't mind telling you that's something I ain't worked out for myself. I don't know how it's done."

"Then get out of the way," was the reply, "and don't bother me. I'm busy."

Tim Keenan continued standing over him, but Scott ignored him. He had managed to get the muzzle in between the jaws on one side, and was trying to get it out between the jaws on the other side. Achieving this, he pried gently and carefully, loosening the jaws a bit at a time, while Matt gently eased out White Fang's mangled neck.

"Stand by to receive your dog," ordered Scott. The card-dealer bent down obediently and got a firm hold on Cherokee.

"Now!" Scott warned, giving the final pry. The dogs were drawn apart, the bulldog struggling vigorously.

"Take him away," Scott commanded, and Tim Keenan dragged Cherokee back into the crowd.

White Fang made several weak efforts to get up. Once he succeeded, but his legs would not hold him, and he slowly wilted back into the snow. His eyes were half closed, and the surface of them was glassy. His jaws were apart, and his tongue hung out, bedraggled and limp. He looked like he had been strangled to death.

Matt examined him. "Just about all in," he announced, "but he's breathin' all right."

Beauty Smith had gotten to his feet and come over to look at White Fang. "Matt, how much is a good sled-dog worth?" Scott asked.

The dog-musher, still on his knees, bent over White Fang, calculated for a moment. "Three hundred dollars," he answered.

"And how much for one that's all chewed up like this one?" Scott asked, nudging White Fang with his foot.

"Half of that," was the dog-musher's judgment. Scott turned upon Beauty Smith.

"Did you hear, Mr. Beast? I'm taking your dog, and I'm giving you a hundred and fifty for him." He opened his wallet and counted out the bills.

Beauty Smith put his hands behind his back, refusing to touch the money. "I ain't a-sellin'," he said.

"Oh, yes, you are," the other assured him. "Because I'm buying. Here's your money. The dog's mine."

Beauty Smith, his hands still behind him, began to back away. Scott sprang toward him, drawing his fist back. The coward cringed. "I've got my rights," he whimpered.

"You've given up your right to own that dog," was the reply. "Are you going to take the money, or do I have to hit you again?"

"All right," Beauty Smith spoke up hastily. "But I take the money under protest," he added. "The dog's worth a fortune. I ain't a-goin' to be robbed. A man's got his rights."

"Correct," Scott answered, giving him the cash. "A man's got his rights. But you're not a man. You're a beast."

"Wait till I get back to Dawson," Beauty Smith threatened. "I'll have the law on you."

"If you open your mouth when you get back to Dawson, I'll have you run out of town. Understand?"

Beauty Smith replied with a grunt.

"Understand?" the other thundered with sudden fury.

"Yes," Beauty Smith grunted, shrinking away.

"Yes, what?"

"Yes, sir," Beauty Smith snarled.

"Look out! He'll bite!" someone shouted, and a chorus of guffawing laughter went up. Scott turned his back on him, and returned to help the dog-musher, who was doctoring White Fang. Some of the men were already leaving; others stood in groups, talking.

Tim Keenan joined one of the groups. "Who's that guy?" he asked.

"Weedon Scott," someone answered.

"And who in hell is Weedon Scott?" the card-dealer demanded.

"Oh, one of them crackerjack minin' experts. He's in with all the big shots. If you want to keep out of trouble, you'll steer clear of him. The Gold Commissioner's a special pal of his."

"I thought he must be somebody important," commented Keenan. "That's why I kept my hands off him at the start."

CHAPTER FIVE
THE DEFIANT

"It's hopeless," Weedon Scott shrugged. He stared at the dog-musher, Matt, who shrugged back. Together they looked at White Fang, bristling and snarling, straining at his chain to get at the sled-dogs. Matt's club had taught the dogs to leave White Fang alone. They were lying down at a distance, apparently unaware of him.

"It's a wolf, and there's no taming it," Weedon Scott announced.

"Oh, I don't know about that," Matt objected. "Might be a lot of dog in 'im. But one thing I know for sure." The dog-musher paused and nodded his head confidently.

"Well, don't keep it a secret," Scott said sharply. "Spit it out. What is it?"

The dog-musher indicated White Fang with a backward thrust of his thumb. "Wolf or dog —he's ben tamed a'ready."

"No!"

"I tell you yes, an' broke to harness. Look close there. D'ye see them marks across the chest?" asked the dog-musher.

Scott confirmed this. "You're right, Matt. He was a sled-dog before Beauty Smith got hold of him."

"And there's not much reason against his bein' a sled-dog again."

"What d'ye think?" Scott asked eagerly. Then he reconsidered, shaking his head. "We've had him two weeks now, and if anything, he's wilder than ever."

"Give 'm a chance," Matt suggested. "Turn 'm loose for a spell."

The other looked at him in amazement.

"Yes," Matt went on, "I know you've tried to, but you didn't take a club."

"You try it, then," challenged Scott.

The dog-musher found a club and went over. White Fang watched the club like a caged lion watches the trainer's whip.

"See 'm keep his eye on that club," Matt said. "That's a good sign. He don't dare tackle me while I got that club handy. He's not all crazy."

As the man's hand approached his neck, White Fang bristled and crouched, snarling. But while he watched the descending hand, he kept an eye on the club in the other. Matt unsnapped the chain from the collar and stepped back.

White Fang could hardly imagine that he was free. Many months had gone by since Beauty Smith had traded for him, months in which he had never known a moment of freedom. He did not know what to think. Perhaps he was about to be the victim of some new mischief of the gods. He walked slowly and cautiously, expecting attack. Staying clear of the watching gods, he walked carefully to the corner of the cabin. Nothing happened. He was plainly confused, and he came back again, pausing a dozen feet away to watch the two men intently.

"Won't he run away?" his new owner asked.

Matt shrugged his shoulders. "Got to take a gamble. Only way to find out is to try."

"Poor devil," Scott murmured pityingly. "What he needs is some show of human kindness," he added, turning and going into the cabin to get a piece of meat. He tossed it to White Fang, who sprang away from it and studied it suspiciously from a distance.

"Hi-yu, Major!" Matt shouted warningly at another dog, but too late.

Major had made a spring for the meat. At the instant his jaws closed on it, White Fang knocked him over. Matt rushed in, but White Fang was quicker. Major staggered to his feet, but the blood from his throat made a widening stain in the snow.

"It's too bad, but it served him right," Scott said hastily. But Matt's foot had already launched a kick at White Fang. There was a leap, a flash of teeth, and a sharp exclamation from Matt. White Fang, snarling fiercely, scrambled backward for several yards, while Matt bent to inspect his leg.

"He got me, all right," he announced, pointing to the torn trousers and long underwear, and the growing red stain.

"I told you it was hopeless, Matt," Scott said in a discouraged voice. "I've thought it over, and now, it's the only thing to do." As he talked, he reluctantly drew his revolver, making sure it was loaded.

"Look here, Mr. Scott," Matt objected. "That dog's been through hell. You can't expect 'm to be a shinin' angel. Give 'm time."

"Look at Major," the other replied.

The dog-musher surveyed the stricken dog. He had sunk down in the bloody snow, rapidly dying.

"Served 'm right. You said so yourself, Mr. Scott. He tried to take White Fang's meat, an' he's dead. That was to be expected. I wouldn't give two hoots for a dog that wouldn't fight for his own meat."

"But look at yourself, Matt. It's all right about the dogs, but we must draw the line somewhere."

"Served me right," Matt argued stubbornly. "What'd I want to kick 'm for? You said yourself that he'd done right. Then I had no right to kick 'm."

"It would be a mercy to kill him," Scott insisted. "He's untamable."

"Now look here, Mr. Scott. Give the poor devil a fightin' chance. He ain't had no chance yet. He's just come through hell, an' this is the first time he's been loose. Give 'm a fair chance, an' if he don't deliver the goods, I'll kill 'm myself. There!"

"God knows I don't want to kill him," Scott answered, putting away the revolver. "We'll let him run loose and see what kindness does for him." He walked over to White Fang and began talking to him gently.

"Better have a club handy," Matt warned. Scott shook his head and kept trying to win White Fang's confidence.

White Fang was suspicious. He had killed this god's dog, bitten his companion god, and that could only gain him some terrible punishment. But he would not show fear. He bristled, eyes vigilant, prepared for anything. The god had no club, so White Fang let him get close. The god's hand was descending upon his head. White Fang grew tense as he crouched, very nervous. The treacherous hands of the gods could give unknown hurts, and he never did like being touched. He snarled more menacingly, not wanting to bite the hand, and held back until his instinct for life took control of him.

Weedon Scott had believed that he was quick enough to avoid any snap or slash. He had yet to learn of White Fang's remarkable quickness. The dog struck as surely and swiftly as a coiled snake.

Scott cried out in surprise, catching his torn hand and holding it tightly in his other. Matt swore and sprang to his side. White Fang crouched down, backed away and bristled, his eyes full of menace. Now he expected a beating as fearful as any he had received from Beauty Smith.

Matt had dashed into the cabin and come out with a rifle. "Here! What are you doing?" Scott cried suddenly.

"Nothin'," he said calmly. "Only goin' to keep that promise I made. I reckon it's up to me to kill 'm as I said I'd do."

"No, you don't!"

"Yes, I do. Watch me."

It was now Weedon Scott's turn to plead, as Matt had when bitten. "You said to give him a chance. Well, give it to him. We've only just started, and we can't quit at the beginning. It served me right. And—look at him!"

White Fang, forty feet away, was snarling blood-curdlingly—not at Scott, but at the dog-musher. "Well, I'll be darned!" exclaimed Matt.

"Look at him," Scott went on hastily. "He knows what a gun is. He's intelligent, and we've got to give that intelligence a chance. Put up the gun."

"All right, I'm willin'," Matt agreed, leaning the rifle against the woodpile. White Fang had ceased snarling. "Let's investigate. Watch."

With that, Matt reached for the rifle, and right then White Fang snarled. He stepped away from the rifle, and White Fang covered his teeth.

"Now, just for fun." Matt took the rifle and began slowly to raise it to his shoulder. White Fang snarled louder as the rifle rose. But just before the rifle pointed at him, he leaped sideways behind the corner of the cabin. Matt stood staring along the sights at the empty space of snow, then put the rifle down solemnly. He turned and looked at his employer.

"I agree with you, Mr. Scott. That dog's too intelligent to kill."

CHAPTER SIX
THE LOVE-MASTER

As White Fang watched Weedon Scott approach, he bristled and snarled defiantly. Twenty-four hours had passed since he had slashed open Scott's now-bandaged hand. In the past White Fang had been given delayed punishments, so punishment was surely coming. After all, he had done the unthinkable, bitten into the holy flesh of a superior god, and something terrible was sure to happen to him. But he would not submit meekly to it.

The god sat down several feet away. White Fang could see no danger in that; when the gods punished, they stood up. Besides, this god had no weapon, nor was White Fang chained. He could escape safely while the god scrambled to his feet. In the meantime, he would wait and see.

The god remained still, and White Fang's snarl slowly died away. Then the god spoke, and the hair rose on White Fang's neck, and he growled. But the god made no hostile moves, and kept talking calmly as White Fang growled. No one had ever talked gently and soothingly to him before. In spite of himself and all his instincts, White Fang began to trust this god. For the first time in his experiences with men, he felt a sense of security.

After a long time, the god got up and went into the cabin. White Fang watched him nervously when he came out. He still had no weapon, nor was his uninjured hand hiding something behind his back. He sat down in the same spot as before, several feet away, then held out a small piece of meat. White Fang perked up and investigated it suspiciously, managing to watch both the meat and the god, ready to spring away at the first sign of hostility.

Still there was no punishment. The god merely held a piece of meat near his nose. Though the meat seemed all right, and was offered to him without threat, he refused to touch it. The gods knew everything, and there was no telling what clever treachery lurked behind that apparently harmless piece of meat. In past experience—especially when he was a sly raider in the Indian village—meat, gods and punishment had often been painfully related.

Eventually, the god tossed the meat on the snow at White Fang's feet. He smelled the meat carefully, but kept his eyes on the god rather than the meat. Nothing happened. He took the meat into his mouth and swallowed

it. Still nothing happened. The god was actually offering him another piece of meat. Again he
refused to take it from the hand, and again it
was tossed to him. This was repeated a number

of times. But eventually the god refused to toss it, and offered it from his hand.

The meat was good, and White Fang was hungry. Very cautiously, he approached the hand. At last he decided to eat the meat from the hand, alertly watching the god, growling to show that he was not to be taken lightly. He ate it, and nothing happened. This happened repeatedly, and without punishment.

He licked his chops and waited. The god kept talking in a kind voice—something new to White Fang. He felt a brand new feeling deep inside, a strange satisfaction. This conflicted with his past experience and instincts, all of which told him that the gods had clever, unknown methods of getting their way.

Ah, he had thought so! There it came now, the god's hand, descending upon his head, likely to hurt him. But the god's voice remained soft and soothing. The hand inspired distrust, but the voice inspired confidence. The conflicting feelings within White Fang were tearing him apart, as he tried to decide what to do.

He compromised. He snarled and bristled and flattened his ears, but he neither snapped nor sprang away. The hand descended nearer. It touched the ends of his upright hair. He shrank down under it. It followed down after him, pressing more closely against him. Almost shivering, he managed to control himself. The hand violated all the instincts of a lifetime of evil experience at the hands of men, but he tried to obey the god's will.

The hand rose and fell again in a patting movement. Every time it lifted, hair rose underneath it. Every time it fell, White Fang's ears flattened and a cavernous growl surged in his throat, announcing urgently that he would retaliate for any hurt. There was no telling when he might know the god's real motive. At any moment, the soft voice might turn to a roar of fury, and that gentle hand could become a viselike grip to hold him, helpless, for punishment.

But the god talked on softly, and the hand rose and fell with harmless pats. White Fang was deeply torn inside. The hand bothered him by going against his urgent need for physical liberty, and yet it did not give physical pain. It was even pleasant, as the patting movement carefully changed to a rubbing behind his ears. Even as he enjoyed the rubbing, his fear continued to torment him.

Matt came out of the cabin, sleeves rolled up, carrying a pan of dirty dishwater. As he was emptying the pan, he saw Weedon Scott patting White Fang. "Well, I'll be darned!" he exclaimed.

At the instant his voice broke the silence, White Fang leaped back, snarling savagely at him.

Matt regarded his employer from the doorway, pretending to disapprove. "If you don't mind my expressin' my feelin's, Mr. Scott, I'll say you're seventeen kinds of a damn fool."

Weedon Scott smiled smugly, got up, and walked over to White Fang. He talked soothingly to him for a moment, then slowly resumed the interrupted patting. White Fang endured it, suspiciously watching the man in the doorway.

Matt continued, "You may be a number one, tip-top minin' expert, all right," the dog-musher proclaimed formally, "but you missed the chance of your life when you was a boy an' didn't run off an' join the circus as a critter-tamer."

White Fang snarled at the sound of his voice, but did not leap away this time from under the hand that was caressing his head and the back of his neck.

It was the beginning of an end for White Fang—the end of the old life with its reign of hate. His new life was much brighter. This took a lot of thought and patience on Weedon

Scott's part, but in White Fang it took a revolution. He had to defy every instinct, experience and thought, even redefine what life meant. This new adjustment was even greater than the one he had made when he came in voluntarily from the Wild and accepted Gray Beaver as his lord. At that time he was a puppy, still easily shaped, but those days were long gone. He was the "Fighting Wolf," fierce, unloving, unlovable, and deeply hardened in his ways. To change now was to tear down and rebuild the habits of a lifetime.

And yet Weedon Scott had the power to remold him. He had gone to the roots of White Fang's nature, reaching parts of him that were nearly dead. One such part was "love." It took the place of "like," which had previously been the upper limit of happiness in his dealings with the gods. The "love" did not come in a day, but grew out of "like." Though he was allowed to remain loose, White Fang did not run away. He liked this new god.

This was certainly better than the life he had lived in the cage of Beauty Smith. Ever since he had left the Wild and crawled to Gray Beaver's feet to receive the expected beating, he had needed the lordship of men. His second return from the Wild, when the long famine was over and there was fish once more in the Indian village, had made that need permanent. And Weedon Scott was a much better god than Beauty Smith.

And so White Fang remained, and took on the duty of guarding his master's property. He prowled around the cabin while the sled-dogs slept, and the first person who visited the cabin at night had to fight him off with a club until Weedon Scott came to the rescue. But White Fang soon learned to tell thieves from honest men by their actions. White Fang left alone anyone who traveled with loud steps directly to the cabin door—though he watched the visitor constantly until the door opened and the master accepted the guest. But the man who peered and sneaked around was immediately judged to be no good, and was sent on a hasty, undignified retreat by White Fang.

To Weedon Scott, it was a matter of justice. Mankind had done the hurt, and owed White Fang a debt. As a man, he felt bound to pay it. So he went out of his way to be especially kind to the "Fighting Wolf." Each day he took time to pet White Fang. At first the dog was suspicious and hostile, but he came to like this petting. One thing that he never outgrew, though, was his habit of growling while being petted. But the growl changed in a way too subtle for a stranger to catch. White Fang's throat had been roughened by many years of making ferocious sounds, and he could not now make soft sounds to express gentleness; he could only modify his growl. Nevertheless, Weedon Scott was sharp enough to catch the new purring note, nearly drowned in the fierceness—the faintest hint of contentment, a sound that only he could hear.

As the days went by, "like" evolved more quickly into "love." White Fang noticed it without really understanding it. For him, "love" was a void in his being, a hungry ache needing to be filled. It was a pain that only the new god's presence could ease. In his presence, "love" gave him joy, a thrilling satisfaction. But when he was away from his god, the hunger for that presence gnawed ceaselessly.

White Fang was changing, in spite of his age and hardened nature. He felt new and strange impulses and feelings. In the past, his actions had been based upon a desire to find comfort and avoid pain, and he had acted accordingly. Now it was different. His new feelings caused him to choose discomfort and pain for his god's sake.

So, in the early morning, instead of roaming

and foraging for food, or lying in a sheltered nook, he would wait for hours on the dreary cabin porch for a sight of the god's face. At night, when the god returned home, White Fang would leave the warm sleeping-place he had burrowed in the snow in order to receive the friendly snap of fingers and the word of greeting. He would even forego meat itself to be with his god, to be petted by him, or to go down to town with him. "Like" had been replaced by "love," which had penetrated parts of him that "like" could not reach. And from inside he returned what was given. This was a warm and radiant love-god.

But White Fang was not outwardly affectionate. He was too old and set in his ways to learn new methods of expression. He had never barked in his life, and he could not now learn to bark a welcome when his god approached. He was never in the way, never overeager in expressing his love. He never ran to meet his god. He waited at a distance—but he always waited. His love took the form of silent, adoring worship. Only by his gaze did he express his love, and by the way his eyes endlessly followed his god's every movement. When his god looked at him and spoke to him, he still felt awkward. He struggled to express physical love, but he was unable.

He adjusted in many ways to his new life. He learned that he must leave his master's dogs alone. Yet his dominant nature asserted itself; he had to establish his dominance. After giving the dogs a few poundings, he had little trouble with them. They got out of his way and obeyed him.

In the same way, he came to understand and accept Matt as a possession of his master. His master rarely fed him; Matt did that. Yet White Fang sensed that the food came from Weedon Scott, and thus considered Matt to be acting for the master. Matt also tried to put him into the harness and make him haul a sled with the other dogs, but failed. Only when Scott put the harness on White Fang and worked him did he understand. It was his master's will that Matt should work him, just as he drove and worked his master's other dogs.

Unlike the Mackenzie toboggans, the Klondike sleds had runners. The dogs were also arranged differently. There was no fan-formation. The dogs worked in single file, one behind the other, attached by double traces. And here, in the Klondike, the leader was indeed the leader, the wisest and strongest dog. The team obeyed him and feared him. It was inevitable that White Fang would quickly become leader. He would accept no less, as Matt learned after much inconvenience. But even though White Fang worked the sled during the day, he did not slack off from guarding his master's property in the night. He was on duty all the time, ever vigilant and faithful, the most valuable of all the dogs.

"Makin' free to speak my mind," Matt said one day, "you was wise, all right, when you paid the price you did for that dog. You clean swindled Beauty Smith on top of pushin' his face in with your fist."

A surge of anger glinted in Weedon Scott's gray eyes, and he muttered savagely, "The beast!"

In the late spring, a great trouble came to White Fang. Without any warning that he could understand, the love-master disappeared. Later, he would remember that the process of packing had preceded the master's disappearance. But that night, he suspected nothing and waited for the master to return. At midnight the chill wind drove him to shelter at the rear of the cabin. There he dozed, half asleep, ears alert for the first sound of the familiar step. By two in the morning, his anxiety drove him out to the cold front porch, where he crouched and waited.

But no master came. In the morning, the

door opened and Matt stepped outside. White Fang gazed at him wistfully. There was no way he could not learn what he wanted to know. The days came and went, but never the master. White Fang, who had never been sick in his life, became ill. He became so sick, so very sick, that Matt finally had to bring him inside the cabin. In writing to his employer, Matt added a postscript about White Fang.

When Weedon Scott read the letter down in Circle City, he came upon the following: "That dam wolf won't work. Won't eat. Ain't got no spunk left. All the dogs is beating him. Wants to know what has become of you, and I don't know how to tell him. Mebbe he is going to die."

Matt was right. White Fang wouldn't eat, and he allowed every dog of the team to punish him. He lay on the cabin floor near the stove, interested in nothing. Matt might talk gently to him or swear at him; it didn't matter. He only turned his dull eyes upon the man and then dropped his head back onto his forepaws again.

One night, when Matt was reading to himself with moving lips and mumbled sounds, he was startled by a low whine from White Fang. The dog was on his feet, ears cocked toward the door, listening intently. A moment later, Matt heard footsteps. The door opened, and Weedon Scott stepped in. They shook hands.

Then Scott looked around the room. "Where's the wolf?" he asked. Then he discovered White Fang, standing where he had been lying, near the stove. He had not rushed forward like the other dogs. He watched and waited.

"Holy smoke!" Matt exclaimed. "Look at 'm wag his tail!"

Weedon Scott strode half across the room toward him, calling him. White Fang came to him, not with a great bound, yet quickly. Something deep inside him awoke. It rose into his eyes, shining forth like a light.

"He never looked at me that way all the time you was gone!" Matt commented.

Weedon Scott did not hear. He was squatting down on his heels, face to face with White Fang and petting him with long, caressing strokes down the neck to the shoulders. And White Fang was growling responsively, the purring note of the growl clearer than ever.

But that was not all. The great love in him, always struggling to express itself, found a new mode of expression. He suddenly thrust his head forward and nudged his way in between the master's arm and body. Confined and almost hidden from view, no longer growling, he continued to nudge and snuggle.

The two men looked at each other. Scott's eyes were shining. "I'll be damned!" Matt exclaimed, awestruck. A moment later, when he had recovered himself, he said, "I always insisted that wolf was a dog. Look at 'm!"

With the return of the love-master, White Fang's recovery was rapid. He spent two nights and a day in the cabin, then went outside. The sled-dogs had forgotten his power. They remembered only a sick, weak dog. As he came out of the cabin, they sprang upon him.

"Talk about your roughhouses," Matt murmured gleefully, looking on from the doorway. "Give 'm hell, you wolf! Give 'm hell!—an' then some!"

White Fang did not need the encouragement. The return of the love-master was enough. Life surged inside him again. He fought from sheer joy, and there could be only one ending. The team dispersed in humiliated defeat, and after dark the dogs came sneaking back, one by one, to bow meekly to his dominance.

Having learned to snuggle, White Fang did it often. Allowing his head to be touched was the final barrier for him, the last instinct of the Wild, the fear of hurt and the trap. Now, with the love-master, he deliberately put himself into a helpless position. It was an expression of perfect trust, of absolute self-surrender.

One night, not long after the return, Scott and Matt sat playing cribbage before bedtime. "Fifteen-two, fifteen-four an' a pair makes six"—Matt was adding up pegs on the cribbage-board—when there was a cry of pain and a sound of snarling outside.

They looked at each other as they started to get up. "The wolf's nailed somebody," Matt said.

A wild scream of fear and anguish made them hurry. "Bring a light!" Scott shouted, as he sprang outside.

Matt followed with the lamp, and by its light they saw a man lying on his back in the snow. His arms were folded across his face and throat, trying to shield himself from White Fang's teeth. And with good reason—White Fang was in a rage, tearing toward his neck. From shoulders to wrists, the coat-sleeves and blue flannel shirt and undershirt were ripped to rags. The arms themselves were terribly slashed, streaming blood.

The two men saw all this instantly.

Immediately, Weedon Scott had White Fang by the throat and was dragging him clear. White Fang struggled and snarled, but made no attempt to bite, quickly quieting down at a sharp word from the master.

Matt helped the wounded man to his feet. The crossed arms lowered, exposing the beastly face of Beauty Smith. The dog-musher let go of him like a man who had picked up something burning. Beauty Smith blinked in the lamplight and looked about him. He saw White Fang, and terror rushed into his face.

At the same moment, Matt noticed two objects lying in the snow. He held the lamp close to them, indicating them with his toe for his employer to see—a steel dog-chain and a stout club.

Weedon Scott saw and nodded. Words were not needed. The dog-musher laid his hand on Beauty Smith's shoulder and faced him about. The thief took off immediately.

In the meantime, the love-master was patting White Fang and talking to him. "Tried to steal you, eh? And you wouldn't have it! Well, well! He made a mistake, didn't he?"

"Ol' Beauty Smith must 'a' thought he had hold of seventeen devils," the dog-musher snickered.

White Fang was still worked up, growling.

Then the hair started lying down. Slowly, the purring note returned.

PART FIVE:
THE TAME

CHAPTER ONE
THE LONG TRAIL

Change was in the air. White Fang sensed a calamity coming. It was more a feeling than an observation, and it came from the gods themselves, who were acting differently than usual.

One night at supper, the dog-musher exclaimed to Scott, "Listen to that, will you!"

Weedon Scott listened, and heard a low, anxious whine, like a low sobbing that had just grown audible. Then came the long sniff, as White Fang reassured himself that his god had not yet gone away alone. "I do believe that wolf's on to you," the dog-musher said.

The mining expert was on edge. "What the devil can I do with a wolf in California?" he demanded.

"That's what I say," Matt answered agreeably. "What the devil can you do with a wolf in California?"

This did not convince Weedon Scott. There was something in Matt's eyes—judgment, perhaps? "Normal dogs would have no hope against him," Scott continued. "He'd kill them on sight. I'd be sued until I was bankrupt, or the authorities would take him away and electrocute him. Maybe both."

"He's a downright murderer, I know," the dog-musher commented, too quickly.

Weedon Scott looked at him suspiciously. "It would never do," he said decisively.

"Nope!" Matt agreed. "Why, you'd have to hire a man 'specially to take care of 'm."

Scott began to believe that Matt was being serious. He nodded cheerfully. The low whine and the searching sniff were heard again at the door.

"There's no denyin' he thinks a hell of a lot of you," Matt said.

The other glared at him in sudden anger. "Damn it all, man! I know my own mind and what's best!"

"I'm agreein' with you, only . . ."

"Only what?" Scott snapped.

"Only . . ." The dog-musher began softly, then changed his mind and showed a rising anger of his own. "Well, you needn't get so worked up about it. Judgin' by your actions, maybe you really don't know your own mind."

Weedon Scott debated with himself for a while, and then said more gently, "You are right, Matt. I don't know my own mind. That's the trouble." He paused, then added, "Why, it would be just ridiculous for me to take that dog along."

"I'm agreein' with you," was Matt's answer, and again his employer was not quite satisfied. "But what I don't get is how on earth he knows you're goin'," the dog-musher continued innocently.

"It's beyond me, Matt," Scott answered, mournfully shaking his head.

Then came the day when, through the open cabin door, White Fang saw the fatal backpack on the floor and the love-master packing things into it. The formerly quiet atmosphere of the cabin was full of unrest and change. Here was proof of what White Fang had already sensed—his god was preparing to leave again. He had been left behind before, so he could expect the same this time.

That night he gave the long wolf-howl, as he had howled in his puppy days, when he fled back to the village to find only a rubbish-heap where Gray Beaver's tepee had stood. He pointed his muzzle to the cold stars and told them his sorrow.

Inside the cabin the two men had just gone to bed. "He's not eatin' again," Matt remarked from his bunk.

There was a grunt from Weedon Scott's bunk, and a stir of blankets. "From the way he was the other time you left," added Matt, "I wouldn't be surprised if this time he died."

The blankets in the other bunk stirred irritably. "Oh, shut up!" Scott cried out through the darkness. "You nag worse than a woman."

"I'm agreein' with you," the dog-musher answered, and Weedon Scott was not quite sure whether Matt had snickered.

The next day White Fang was even more anxious. He stayed at his master's heels whenever he left the cabin, and haunted the front porch when Scott remained inside. Through the open door he could see the luggage piling up. Matt was rolling up the master's blankets and fur robe. White Fang watched and whined. Later, two Indians arrived. He watched them closely as they carried the luggage down the hill with Matt, but he did not follow them. The master was still in the cabin. After a time, Matt returned. Scott came to the door and called White Fang inside.

"You poor devil," he said gently, rubbing White Fang's ears and tapping his spine. "I'm hitting the long trail, old man, where you cannot follow. Now give me a last goodbye growl."

But White Fang refused to growl. Instead, with a wistful, searching look, he burrowed his head out of sight between the master's arm and body. From the Yukon arose the hoarse bellowing of a river steamboat. "There she blows!" Matt cried. "You've got to cut it short. Be sure and lock the front door. I'll go out the back. Get moving!"

The two doors slammed at the same moment, and Weedon Scott waited out front for Matt. From inside the door came a low whining and sobbing, then long, deep-drawn sniffs. "Take good care of him, Matt," Scott said, as they started down the hill. "Write and let me know how he gets along."

"Sure," the dog-musher answered. "But listen to that, will you!"

Both men stopped. White Fang was howling as dogs howl when their masters lie dead. His voice was utter woe, his cry bursting upward in heartbreaking rushes, then dying down into quivering misery, then repeating.

The *Aurora* was the first steamboat of the year sailing for the Outside—as men of the North called everyplace else—and her decks were jammed with adventurers and gold seekers, most of whom had failed. All were as eager now to get Outside as they had originally been to reach the North.

Near the gangplank, Scott was shaking hands with Matt, who was preparing to go ashore. But Matt's hand went limp in the other's grasp as his gaze fixed on something behind him. Scott turned to see.

Sitting on the deck several feet away and watching wistfully was White Fang. The dog-musher swore softly in awe. Scott could only look in wonder. "Did you lock the front door?" Matt demanded.

The other nodded and asked, "How about the back?"

"You just bet I did," was Matt's fervent reply. White Fang sat still. "I'll have to take 'm ashore with me," Matt added. He took a couple of steps toward White Fang, but the wolf-dog slid away from him. The dog-musher rushed him, and White Fang dodged between the legs of a group of men. Ducking, turning, he slid about the deck, avoiding capture.

But when the love-master spoke, White Fang came promptly.

"Won't come to the hand that's fed 'm all these months," the dog-musher muttered resentfully. "And you—you ain't never fed 'm after them first days. I'm blamed if I can see how he reckons you're the boss."

Scott, who had been patting White Fang,

suddenly pointed out fresh cuts on his muzzle, and a gash between the eyes. Matt bent over and passed his hand along White Fang's belly, then exclaimed, "We plumb forgot the window. He's all cut an' gouged underneath. Must 'a' butted clean through it, b'gosh!"

Weedon Scott was not listening. He thought rapidly. The *Aurora*'s whistle hooted one last time. Men were scurrying down the gangplank to the shore. Matt loosened his bandanna and started to put it around White Fang's neck. Scott grasped the dog-musher's hand. "Goodbye, Matt, old man. No need to write about the wolf. You see, I've . . . !"

"What!" the dog-musher exploded. "You don't mean to say . . .?"

"But I do. Here's your bandanna. I'll write to you about him."

Matt paused halfway down the gangplank. "He'll never stand the climate!" he shouted back. "Unless you clip 'm in warm weather!"

The gangplank was hauled in, and the *Aurora* swung out from the bank. Weedon Scott waved a last goodbye. Then he turned and bent over White Fang. "Now growl, damn you," he said, as he patted the responsive head and rubbed the flattening ears.

CHAPTER TWO
THE SOUTHLAND

White Fang walked off the steamer in San Francisco. He was appalled. He associated power with the gods, and in San Francisco the white man-gods seemed more impressive than ever. Towering buildings replaced the log cabins he had known. The streets were crowded with perils: wagons, carts, automobiles; great, straining horses pulling huge trucks; and monstrous cable cars, hooting and clanging, screeching like the lynxes he had known in the northern woods.

Behind all this was man, controlling it all, all-powerful. White Fang was awed, stunned and afraid. He felt as small and puny as the day he first came in from the Wild to Gray Beaver's village. And there were so many gods! Their numbers made him dizzy. The thunder of the streets assaulted his ears; the endless rush and movement bewildered him. He felt more dependent than ever on the love-master, and stayed close at his heels.

But White Fang was to have only a brief, terrifying vision of the city, one that would haunt him for a long time to come, like a bad dream. The master chained him in the midst of a heap of luggage in a baggage-car. Here a squat and brawny god was in charge, hurling trunks and boxes about with much noise, smashing and commotion. In this inferno of luggage, the master had deserted White Fang, or so he thought until he smelled out the master's canvas clothes-bags alongside of him, and took up guard duty over them.

"'Bout time you come," growled the god of the car, an hour later, when Weedon Scott appeared at the door. "That dog of yourn won't let me near your stuff."

White Fang emerged from the car. He was astonished. The nightmare city was gone. The car had been no more than a room, and when he had entered it, the city had surrounded him. Now the city and its roar had disappeared. Before him was smiling country, streaming with sunshine and lazy calm. But he had little time to marvel at the transformation. The gods were full of strange doings and appearances, more of which were about to take place, and all of which he must accept.

There was a carriage waiting. A man and a woman approached the master. The woman's arms went out and clutched the master around the neck—a hostile act! The next moment, Weedon Scott had torn loose from the embrace and closed with White Fang, who had become a snarling, raging demon.

"It's all right, Mother," Scott was saying, as he kept tight hold of White Fang and calmed him down. "He thought you were going to injure me, and he wouldn't stand for it. It's all right. He'll learn soon enough."

"And in the meantime, I may be permitted to love my son when his dog is not around," she laughed, though she was pale from fright. She looked at White Fang, who snarled and bristled and glared menacingly.

"He'll learn right now," Scott said. He spoke softly to White Fang until he had quieted him. Then his voice became firm.

"Down, sir! Down with you!" The master had taught him this before, and White Fang obeyed, though reluctantly and sullenly.

"Now, Mother." Scott opened his arms to her, but kept his eyes on White Fang. "Down!" he warned. "Down!"

White Fang, bristling silently, sank back and watched the hostile act repeated. But no harm came of it, nor of the embrace from the strange man-god that followed. Then the clothes bags were taken into the carriage, followed by the strange gods and the love-master. White Fang ran vigilantly behind, bristling up to the running horses from time to time to warn them not to harm his god.

After fifteen minutes, the carriage swung

in through a stone gateway and onto the grounds of a beautiful estate. Its broad lawns and sturdy trees led up to a large house with many windows. The carriage had barely entered the grounds when White Fang was attacked by an angry, bright-eyed, sharp-muzzled sheep dog. It got between him and the master, cutting him off. Without warning, White Fang bristled and went into his silent, deadly rush. But it was never completed. He halted with awkward abruptness when he realized the situation. This was a female, and the law and every instinct of his kind forbade him from attacking a female.

The female sheep dog, of course, had no such instinctive restraint. Quite the opposite, for her breed had an instinctive fear of the Wild—especially wolves. To her, White Fang was a raider who had inherited the instinct to prey upon her flocks, and had attacked those of her ancestors, far into the dim past. And so, as White Fang abandoned his rush and braced, she sprang on him. He snarled involuntarily as he felt her teeth in his shoulder, but made no effort to hurt her. Instead, he backed away self-consciously and tried to dodge and curve around her. But she stayed in his way.

"Here, Collie!" called the strange man in

the carriage.

Weedon Scott laughed. "Never mind, Father. It is good discipline. White Fang will have to learn many things, and it's just as well that he begins now. He'll adjust, all right."

The carriage drove on, and still Collie blocked White Fang's way. He tried to outrun her by circling back and forth across the lawn and the driveway, but she stayed between him and the house, facing him with two rows of gleaming teeth.

White Fang caught glimpses of the carriage disappearing among the trees, carrying the master away. The situation was desperate. He circled once, more, failed to evade her, and then suddenly he turned upon her. It was his old fighting trick. He struck her squarely, shoulder to shoulder, bowling her over. She had been going so fast that she rolled several times with the impact. In hurt pride and indignation, she tried to stop, clawing up gravel and crying out shrilly.

White Fang did not wait. The way was clear, and that was all he had wanted. She took after him in full cry. Now the course was straight, and when it came to real running, she could not equal White Fang. She ran frantically, noisily straining to the utmost. He slid smoothly away from her, silently and effortlessly, gliding like a ghost over the ground.

As he came to the covered carriageway near the house, he found the master exiting the carriage. Suddenly he became aware of an attack from the side—a deer-hound rushing him. He tried to face it, but he was going too fast, and the house was too near. It rammed into his side, rolling him clear over. He came up in a fury, ears back, lips quivering, and his teeth clipped together as the fangs barely missed the hound's soft throat.

The master was coming, but was too far away to intervene. It was Collie that saved the hound's life. Just as White Fang sprang in to deliver the fatal stroke, the humiliated sheep-dog plowed like a tornado into this enemy from the Wild. She hit him at a right angle in mid-spring, bowling him over again.

The next moment the master arrived, and held White Fang with one hand while the father called off the dogs.

"I say, this is a pretty warm reception for a poor, lone wolf from the Arctic," the master said, while White Fang calmed down under his caressing hand. "In all his life he's only known to have been knocked off his feet once, and here he's been rolled twice in thirty seconds."

The carriage had driven away, and other

strange gods had come out of the house. Some of these stood respectfully at a distance, but two of them, women, performed the hostile act of clutching the master around the neck. White Fang, however, was beginning to tolerate it. No harm seemed to come of it, nor were the gods making threatening sounds. These gods also tried to reach out to White Fang, but he warned them off with a snarl. The master did so also, aloud. White Fang stayed close against the master's legs, getting reassuring pats on the head.

The hound received the command. "Dick! Lie down, sir!" He went up the steps and lay down on one side of the porch, still growling and keeping a sullen watch on the intruder. One of the woman-gods was hugging and petting Collie, but the sheep-dog remained perplexed and worried. She whined her outrage and nervousness, confident that her gods were making a mistake by allowing a wolf so near.

All the gods started up the steps to enter the house. White Fang followed closely at the master's heels. Dick growled as they crossed the porch, and White Fang bristled and growled back. "Take Collie inside and leave the two of them to fight it out," suggested Scott's father. "After that they'll be friends."

"White Fang will show his friendship by being chief mourner at Dick's funeral," laughed the master.

The elder Scott looked with disbelief, first at White Fang, then at Dick, and finally at his son. "You mean . . .?"

Weedon nodded his head. "I mean just that. Dick would be dead in one minute. Maybe two minutes at the most." He turned to White Fang. "Come on, you wolf. It's you that'll have to come inside."

White Fang walked stiff-legged up the steps and across the porch. He kept his tail rigidly erect, remained alert for a flank attack from Dick, and at the same time prepared for whatever fierce, unknown thing might pounce on him from inside the house. But nothing did, and he scouted the inside carefully, finding no threat. Then he lay down with a contented grunt at the master's feet, watching everything, ever ready to spring to his feet and fight for his life against whatever terrors and traps surely must be hiding in such a dwelling.

CHAPTER THREE
THE GOD'S DOMAIN

White Fang was adaptable by nature, so he quickly made himself at home at Judge Scott's place. He had no further serious trouble with the dogs of Sierra Vista, as the estate was named. They knew more about the ways of the Southland gods than he did. And when he accompanied the gods into the house, this showed them that the gods allowed his presence; and so must they.

Dick had to go through a few stiff formalities at first, but soon he calmly accepted White Fang as a dog that belonged there. At first, Dick wanted them to be good friends, but White Fang was not receptive. All he wanted from other dogs was privacy, so he snarled Dick away. He had learned in the North to leave his master's dogs alone, and he insisted on being alone. After being ignored for awhile, good-natured Dick finally gave up, and White Fang got his wish.

Collie was not so accommodating. The gods' law might require her to accept him, but it did not mean that she had to leave him in peace. Her feud with his kind was ancient and deep; the destroyed sheep-flocks would not soon be forgotten. Compelled by this burning instinct of duty, she continued the ancient feud by making his life miserable in petty ways. She took advantage of her gender. He would not attack her, but she was too persistent to ignore. When she rushed at him, he turned his fur-protected shoulder to her sharp teeth and walked proudly away. When she was too insistent, he avoided her, his expression patient and bored. Sometimes she got him a nip in the hindquarters and caused him to make a hasty and undignified retreat, but not often. Mostly, he ignored and avoided her.

White Fang had a lot to learn. Life in Sierra Vista was much more complicated than life in the Northland. First, he had to learn the master's family, and life with Gray Beaver had prepared him for this. As Mit-sah and Kloo-kooch had belonged to Gray Beaver, all those living in the house at Sierra Vista belonged to the love-master.

This family was very different. Sierra Vista was much larger than Gray Beaver's tepee, and there were many persons to consider. There were Judge Scott and his wife, the master's two sisters, Beth and Mary, and the master's immediate family: his wife, Alice, and his two children, Weedon and Maud, aged four and six, respectively. White Fang came to understand their family ties in terms of his master. By watching the master's actions and speech toward them, even his tone of voice, he learned where each person stood in the master's favor and affection. This guided his treatment of them. What was of value to the master was of value to him, and anything loved by the master was to be loved by White Fang—and guarded carefully.

It was so with the two children. He remembered very well the cruelty and tyranny of the children in the Indian villages, whose hands gave hurt. When Weedon and Maud had first approached him, he growled warningly and looked mean. A swat from the master and a sharp word told him to permit their petting, though he growled under their tiny hands—a growl with no softness. Later, he observed that the boy and girl were greatly valued by the master, and from then on he let them pet him on their own. He was never affectionate, but endured the children as one would a painful operation. When he had had enough, he got up and stalked away. After a time, he even grew to like them and to wait for them to come to him. Eventually, he even looked pleased when they came and curiously sorry when they left him for other amusements.

All of this took time. After the children,

White Fang's highest regard was for Judge Scott, because the master obviously valued the judge. This god was not affectionate, but he did sometimes favor White Fang with a look or a word of recognition. White Fang liked to lie at the judge's feet on the porch when he read the newspaper, but only when the master was not around. When the master appeared, all other beings ceased to exist for White Fang. White Fang allowed all the members of the family to pet him, but his love-growl and snuggles were reserved for the love-master alone.

White Fang also learned to tell the family apart from the household servants, who feared him. He regarded them neutrally, as possessions of his master, who must not be attacked. They cooked and washed and cleaned for the master, so he saw them as he had seen Matt up in the Klondike, as accessories of the household.

Outside the household there was even more for White Fang to learn. The master's domain seemed wide and complex, yet it reached only to the county road. Outside was the common domain of all gods—the roads and streets. Inside other fences were the particular domains of other gods. Many laws governed all these things, but he could learn them only by experience. Therefore, he obeyed his natural impulses until they went against some law. When this happened a few times, he learned the law and obeyed it thereafter.

The most powerful aspect of his education was a light swat or a harsh word from the master. White Fang's love was so great that a mild scolding of this type hurt him far more than any beating Gray Beaver or Beauty Smith had ever given him. Their beatings had hurt only his flesh; his spirit had still raged, splendid and invincible. The master's swats were always too gentle to hurt his flesh, but his disapproval made White Fang's spirit wilt. In fact, he was rarely punished. White Fang knew by his master's voice whether he had done right or wrong, and he adjusted his actions accordingly.

In the Northland, the only domesticated animal was the dog. All other animals lived in the Wild and were fair game for any dog that could kill them. All his life, White Fang had foraged among live things for food. He was soon to learn that in the Santa Clara Valley of the Southland, it was different. Strolling around the corner of the house in the early morning, he came upon a chicken that had escaped from the chicken-yard. To him, birds were food. A couple of leaps, a flash of teeth, and a frightened squawk, and then he was devouring the adventurous, tasty bird.

Later in the day, he chanced upon another stray chicken near the stables. One of the stable men ran to the rescue. He did not know White Fang's history, so he picked up a light buggy-whip. At the first cut of the whip, White Fang left the chicken for the man. A club might have stopped White Fang, but not a whip. As the wolf-dog silently rushed forward, he got but ignored a second cut from the whip, then leaped for the throat. The man cried out in shock and staggered backward, dropping the whip and shielding his throat with his arms. White Fang's teeth ripped his forearm open to the bone.

The man was badly frightened. White Fang's silence was scarier even than his ferocity. The man continued to shield his face and throat with the wounded arm during his retreat. If Collie had not shown up, the man might have died. But she saved his life as she had saved Dick's. Infuriated, she rushed in on White Fang. She had been right all along, unlike the ignorant gods, who had foolishly let the ancient marauder in. All her suspicions were justified.

The stable man escaped into the stables. White Fang tried to evade Collie, but unlike her normal habit, she did not let up on him after a time. Instead, she grew more excited and angry every moment until, finally, White Fang flung dignity to the winds and simply fled across the fields.

"He'll learn to leave chickens alone," the master said. "But I can't give him the lesson until I catch him in the act."

Two nights later came the act, but on a larger scale than the master had anticipated. White Fang had studied the chicken-yards and the birds' habits. At night after the chickens had gone to roost, he climbed to the top of a pile of lumber. From there he got onto the roof of one of the chicken-houses, found an opening, and dropped to the ground inside. A moment later he was inside the house, and the slaughter began.

In the morning, when the master came out onto the porch, he saw fifty dead white Leghorn hens, laid out in a row by the stable man. He whistled softly to himself in surprise and admiration. He also saw White Fang, who looked proud of a good night's work. The master's lips tightened as he faced the disagreeable task. Then he talked to the wolf-dog in a voice full of godlike anger. He also held White Fang's nose down to the slain hens and swatted him thoroughly.

White Fang never raided a chicken-roost again; it was clearly against the law. Then the master took him into the chicken-yards. When he saw the live food fluttering about under his very nose, White Fang's natural impulse was to spring upon it. He obeyed the impulse, but was halted by the master's voice. They continued in the yards for half an hour, and each time White Fang showed signs of losing control, the master's voice again stopped him. In this way, he learned the law: he must leave the chickens alone.

"You can never cure a chicken-killer." Judge Scott shook his head sadly at lunch, when his son told of the lesson he had given White Fang. "Once they've got the habit and the taste of blood . . ." Again, he shook his head sadly.

Weedon Scott did not agree with his father. "I'll tell you what I'll do," he challenged finally. "I'll lock White Fang in with the chickens all afternoon."

"But think of the chickens," objected the judge.

"And furthermore," the son went on, "for every chicken he kills, I'll pay you a one-dollar gold-piece."

"But what will Father pay if he loses?" asked Beth. "If he loses this bet, he should also have to pay something."

Her sister agreed with her, and a chorus of approval arose from around the table. Judge Scott nodded his head in agreement.

"All right." Weedon Scott pondered for a moment. "And if, at the end of the afternoon, White Fang hasn't harmed a chicken, for every ten minutes of the time he has spent in the yard, you will have to say to him, slowly and seriously, 'White Fang, you are smarter than I thought.'"

The family hid to watch the performance, but it was boring. Locked in the yard and abandoned there by the master, White Fang lay down and went to sleep. Once he got up and walked over to the trough for a drink of water. The chickens might as well not exist. At four o'clock, he took a running jump onto the roof of the chicken-house and leaped to the ground outside, sauntering toward the house with his usual dignity. He had learned the law. On the porch, to his family's amused delight, Judge Scott paid his bet. Face to face with White Fang, he said solemnly, sixteen times, "White Fang, you are smarter than I thought."

What most often got White Fang into trouble were the many complex laws that now applied. He had to learn that he must not touch other gods' chickens. Then there were cats, and rabbits, and turkeys, all of which he must leave alone. In fact, at one point, the law seemed to be that he must leave all live things alone. During this time, a quail could flutter up under his nose, unharmed. Tense and trembling with eagerness, he mastered his instinct and remained still, obedient to the will of the gods.

And then one day, out in the back pasture, he saw Dick scare up and chase a jackrabbit. The master was looking on and did not interfere; he actually encouraged White Fang to join in the chase. And thus he learned that there was no law protecting jackrabbits. In the end, he worked out the entire law. He must remain at peace, if not friendship, with all domestic animals. Other animals—such as squirrels and quail and cottontail rabbits—were creatures of the Wild. They were outside the gods' protection, and lawful prey for any dog.

The variety of life in the Santa Clara Valley was far greater than that of the simple Northland. White Fang now had to adjust to a thousand different forms and faces of life. For example, meat hung within reach at butcher shops, but he must not touch it. The master visited houses with cats, which he had better leave alone. There were dogs everywhere that snarled at him, yet he must not attack them. Most of all, on the crowded sidewalks there were many people. They would stop and look at him, point him out, and worst of all, pat him. And he must endure it all. In so doing, he gained confidence, and received the attentions of strange gods with calm, lofty arrogance. Something about him seemed to warn them not to take liberties, though, and they patted him on the head and passed on, pleased with their own daring.

White Fang found some aspects of his new life especially difficult. As he ran behind the carriage in the outskirts of San Jose, a group of small boys made a habit of throwing rocks at him. He knew that he was forbidden to chase and punish them. This violated his instinct of self-preservation, but he obeyed. He was becoming tame and ready for civilization.

Nevertheless, White Fang was not quite satisfied with this. He had an inner sense of justice, which led him to resent the unfairness of the children who threw rocks at him when he could not fight back. However, he had forgotten a portion of the law: the agreement between him and the gods required them to keep him safe, and Weedon Scott was not blind. One day the master sprang from the carriage, whip in hand, and gave the rock-throwers a thrashing. The rock-throwing ended. White Fang understood and was satisfied.

He had another such experience one day. On the way to town, hanging around a cross-roads saloon, were three dogs that made a practice of rushing out upon him when he went by. Knowing how deadly a fighter White Fang could be, the master had repeatedly taught him the law: he must not fight.

This posed a problem whenever they passed the saloon. White Fang's snarls kept them at bay after the first rush, but they trailed and harassed him. He took this for the insult that it was. This went on for some time, and the men at the saloon even began to egg the dogs on. One day they went too far and openly sent the dogs to attack him. The master stopped the carriage.

"Go to it," he said to White Fang.

White Fang could not believe it. He looked at the master, and he looked at the dogs. Then he looked back eagerly and questioningly at the master. The master nodded his head and spoke firmly. "Go get 'em, old fellow. Sic 'em."

White Fang no longer hesitated. He

turned and leaped silently among his three enemies. There was a great snarling and growling, a clashing of teeth, and a flurry of bodies. The dust of the road hid the battle.

At the end of several minutes, two dogs were struggling and bleeding their lives away in the dirt, their throat-veins bitten open. The third was in full flight over a ditch and across a field, but he was not safe. White Fang followed him, sliding over the ground in wolf fashion and with a wolf's speed. In the center of the field, he dragged down and killed the last dog.

When word of this triple killing got out, most of White Fang's dog troubles ended. From then on, the men of the Santa Clara Valley kept their dogs clear of the Fighting Wolf.

CHAPTER FOUR
THE CALL OF KIND

The months came and went in the Southland. White Fang was happy and healthy. With plenty of food, no work, and lots of human kindness, he flourished like a flower planted in good soil.

He missed the snow. The Southland seemed like an abnormally long summer, and the summer was hotter than those White Fang was used to. He suffered from it, feeling restless longings for the North.

He remained somehow different and apart from other dogs. He knew and obeyed the law better than most, but he gave the impression of lurking ferocity, as though the wolf of the Wild inside him merely slept. First there had been his puppyhood, with Lip-lip and the puppy-pack, and later had come his fighting days with Beauty Smith. Both experiences had taught him to dislike and avoid other dogs. Since he backed off from his own kind, he had clung more to humans. For their part, all Southland dogs were suspicious of him. He brought out their instinctive fear of the Wild, and they greeted him with aggressive, snarling hatred. He rarely had to use his teeth on them. Usually, the sight of his naked fangs and writhing lips was enough to make even the most threatening dog back off.

Collie was White Fang's one trial in life. She gave him no peace. She would not befriend him, despite all the master's efforts. Even before he had killed the chickens, she had decided he was no good. In her mind, he had then proven her exactly right, and she never forgave him. Her sharp, nervous snarl was never far from his ears. She followed him around like a policeman, and if he even glanced curiously at a pigeon or a chicken, she made a lot of angry noise. His best tactic was to ignore her by lying down and pretending to sleep, which confused and silenced her. But except for her annoying watchfulness, he no longer lived in a hostile environment. Even his dread of the unknown faded.

White Fang had never been very demonstrative. Beyond the snuggling and softening of his growl, he had no way to show love. In time he learned two more ways.

In the past, when the gods had laughed at him, it had driven him into a rage. The love-master sometimes laughed good-naturedly at him, and he felt the old anger stirring, but it could not match his love for the master. When he tried to remain dignified, the master only laughed harder, until finally White Fang had to join him. He developed a sort of open-jawed smile, with eyes more full of love than humor, which was as close to a laugh as he could ever come. In the same way, he learned to play-wrestle with the master, to allow himself to be tumbled over. He would put on a display of anger, snapping with mock deadliness, but he never forgot himself. The snaps always closed on air. At the end of a wrestle, they would suddenly square off and glare at one another a few feet apart. Then, just as suddenly, they would begin to laugh. The master would always hug White Fang, and the latter would give his love-growl.

But White Fang allowed nobody else to romp in this way with him. If they tried, his bristle and snarl were not playful at all. He might allow the master such liberties, but that did not mean he had to become a common dog, everyone's toy. He had too much dignity and love for that.

The master often went out on horseback, and one of White Fang's chief duties was to accompany him. In the North he had pulled a sled, but here dogs did not haul burdens. No matter how long the master rode, White Fang was never worn out. Even at the end of a ride of fifty miles, the smooth, effortless, tireless stride of the wolf would keep him proudly in front. And through riding, White Fang learned one other mode of expression, though he used it only twice in his whole life.

The first time occurred when the master was trying to teach a frisky horse how to open and close gates without his having to dismount. Several times he brought the horse up to the gate, but each time it reared away in fear. As Scott's horse grew more nervous, he put the spurs on his boots into it. This brought its forelegs back to earth, but the horse then began to buck. White Fang watched anxiously until he could no longer contain himself. He sprang in front of the horse and, for the first time in his entire life, barked out a savage warning.

With the master's encouragement, he kept trying to bark again after that incident, but only once did he succeed, and the master was not around to hear it. They were out in the pasture, the master on horseback, when a jackrabbit sprang up at the horse's feet. The horse reared violently, stumbled and fell to earth, throwing the master and breaking his leg.

White Fang's first impulse was to spring for the horse's throat in rage, but the master's voice stopped him, as he checked to see what his injury was. When he realized that his leg was broken, he gave a command: "Home! Go home!"

White Fang was reluctant to desert him. The master thought of writing a note, but had nothing to write with. He gave White Fang the command again: "Go home!" The wolf-dog regarded him wistfully, started away, then returned and whined softly. The master talked to him gently, but seriously. White Fang listened with painful intensity.

"That's all right, old fellow, you just run along home," said Scott. "Go on home and tell them what's happened to me. Home with you, you wolf! Get along home!" White Fang knew the meaning of "home," and though he did not understand the remainder of the master's language, he knew he must go home. He turned and trotted reluctantly away.

Then he stopped, undecided, and looked back over his shoulder. "Go home!" came the sharp command, and this time he obeyed. He leaped into his wolf-stride and soon vanished from the master's sight.

The family was on the porch, enjoying the cool afternoon breeze, when White Fang came in among them. He was panting and covered with dust. "Weedon's back," Weedon's mother announced.

The children ran with glad cries to meet

White Fang. He avoided them and moved along the wide, wrap-around porch, but they cornered him against a rocking-chair and the railing. He growled and tried to push by them. Their mother looked apprehensively in their direction.

"I confess, he makes me nervous around the children," said Weedon Scott's wife. "I am afraid that he will turn upon them unexpectedly some day."

Growling savagely, White Fang sprang out of the corner, knocking the children over. The mother called them to her and comforted them, telling them not to bother White Fang.

"A wolf is a wolf!" commented Judge Scott. "You cannot trust one."

"But he is not all wolf," interposed Beth, standing up for her absent brother.

"You have only Weedon's opinion for that," rejoined the judge. "He thinks that there is some dog blood in White Fang. But as he will tell you himself, he knows nothing about it. As for his appearance . . ."

He did not finish his sentence. White Fang stood before him, growling fiercely.

"Go away! Lie down, sir!" Judge Scott commanded.

White Fang turned to the love-master's wife and took her dress in his teeth. She screamed with fright as he dragged on it until a piece of frail fabric tore away. He now had everyone's attention, so he ceased growling and stood, head up, looking into their faces. His throat worked soundlessly as he tried to somehow say what was on his mind.

"I hope he is not going mad," said Weedon's mother. "I told Weedon that I was afraid the warm climate would be hard on an Arctic animal."

"He's trying to speak, I do believe," Beth announced.

At this moment a form of speech came to White Fang. Out rushed a great burst of barking.

"Something has happened to Weedon," his wife said decisively. Soon they were all on their feet, and White Fang ran down the steps, looking back for them to follow. For the second and last time in his life, he had barked and made himself understood.

After this event, the hearts of the Sierra Vista people warmed to him, and even the stable man, whose arm he had slashed, admitted that he was a wise dog, wolf or no wolf. Judge Scott alone continued to consider him a wolf. He dug through various reference books in an effort to prove his point, much to everyone's annoyance.

The days came and went, streaming their unbroken sunshine over the Santa Clara Valley. But as White Fang's second winter in the Southland came on, something changed. Collie's nips no longer felt as sharp. She was playful. He forgot the trouble she had caused him, and tried to be solemnly playful. But he played so solemnly that he only looked ridiculous.

One day the master was planning to ride, his horse saddled and waiting at the door. As White Fang waited for the master, Collie tried to entice him away. White Fang was indecisive, but ultimately there was something even deeper inside him than all the laws, customs, and love he had learned. Finally, Collie nipped him and scampered off, and he turned and followed. She led him on a long chase through the back pasture into the woods.

The master rode alone that day. In the woods, White Fang ran with Collie, as his mother Kiche and old One Eye had run many years before in the silent Northland forest.

CHAPTER FIVE
THE SLEEPING WOLF

At about this time, the newspapers were full of the daring escape of a ferocious convict from San Quentin prison. Something had been wrong with Jim Hall from birth, and the harsh treatment he had received from society when he was growing up had not helped matters. In short, he was a terrible human beast.

In prison he showed no signs whatsoever of reforming. Punishment never broke his spirit. The more fiercely he fought, the more harshly society handled him, and this, of course, only made him fiercer. The prison guards used straitjackets, starvation, beatings and clubbings on him. Society had been trying to mold him with these tools since he was an easily-shaped little boy in a San Francisco slum, and they still did no good.

During Jim Hall's third term in prison, he encountered a guard that was almost as beastly as he. The guard treated him unfairly, lied about him to the warden, made him lose his good-behavior credits, and picked on him. The only difference between them was that the guard carried keys and a revolver, while Jim Hall had only his naked hands and his teeth.

One day Jim Hall sprang upon the guard. He used those hands and teeth on the hated guard's throat, just like any jungle animal. After this, he spent three years in the iron tomb of solitary confinement. He never saw the sky or the sunshine. He knew day only as a twilight, and night only as a black silence. He had no human contact. When his food was shoved in to him, he growled like a wild animal. He hated all things. For days and nights he bellowed his rage at the universe. Then for weeks and months he made no sound. He was as fearful a monster as any maddened brain had ever imagined.

The guards said escape was impossible, but one night the cell-tomb was found empty. A trail of three dead guards marked his path through the prison to the outer walls. He had killed silently with his hands.

He was armed with the guards' weapons, and the authorities put a huge bounty on his head. Greedy farmers hunted him with shotguns. His blood-money might pay off a mortgage or send a son to college. Public-spirited citizens got out their rifles and went out after him. A pack of bloodhounds followed the trail left by his bleeding feet. And the detective-hounds of the law, the animals society paid to fight, clung to his trail night and day, using all the tools at their disposal.

Sometimes when they came upon him, the men either faced him like heroes, or stampeded through barbed-wire fences to the delight of those reading the story in the morning paper. After such encounters, the dead and wounded were carted back to the towns, and their places filled by other men eager for the manhunt.

And then Jim Hall disappeared. The bloodhounds' trail went cold. Harmless ranchers in remote valleys were held up by armed men and ordered to identify themselves. The supposed remains of Jim Hall were "discovered" on a dozen mountainsides by men greedy for blood-money.

The people of Sierra Vista kept up with the newspapers, more from anxiety than from curious interest. The women were afraid. Judge Scott pooh-poohed and laughed, but maybe he should not have, for he had been the one to sentence Jim Hall. The criminal had two prior convictions, so the judge sentenced him to fifty years in prison. At his sentencing, Jim Hall had raged about how he had been mistreated all his life. It had taken half a dozen police to silence him. He vowed revenge upon Judge Scott, whom he saw as the source of all injustice.

For once, Jim Hall had been right about one small thing. He was innocent, at least of the crime for which he was sentenced. He had been "railroaded," as they said in that time— framed. Judge Scott had no idea that the police had faked the evidence and lied under oath in court. But Jim Hall, too, was mistaken. The beast-man did not realize that Judge Scott had been fooled by a conspiracy. Jim Hall believed that the judge had helped the police to do him a great wrong.

White Fang knew nothing of courts and criminals. But he and Alice, the master's wife, had a secret. Each night, after Sierra Vista had gone to bed, she arose and let White Fang in, so he could sleep in the big hall. White Fang was not supposed to be allowed to sleep in the house, so early each morning, she slipped down and let him out before the family was awake.

On one such night, while the whole house slept, White Fang awoke and lay very quietly. He smelled a strange god's presence. His ears heard sounds of the strange god's movements.

As ever, White Fang was silent. The strange god walked softly, but White Fang walked even more softly, for he had no clothes to rub against the flesh of his body. He followed silently. In the Wild he had hunted ter-

rified live meat, and he knew the advantage of surprise.

The strange god paused at the foot of the great staircase and listened, and White Fang watched and waited in deathly stillness. Up that staircase the way led to the love-master and to the love-master's dearest possessions. White Fang bristled, but waited. The strange god's foot lifted. He was beginning the climb.

Then it was that White Fang struck. He gave no warning, no snarl. His spring took him airborne and onto the strange god's back. White Fang clung with his forepaws to the man's shoulders, at the same time burying his fangs into the back of the man's neck. He clung for a moment, long enough to drag the god over backward. Together they crashed to the floor. White Fang leaped clear, and, as the man struggled to rise, moved in again with his slashing fangs.

Sierra Vista awoke in alarm. The noise from downstairs was like twenty battling fiends. There were revolver shots. A man's voice screamed once in horror and anguish. There was a great snarling and growling, and over it all arose a smashing and crashing of furniture and glass.

Then, almost as quickly as it had arisen, the commotion died away. The struggle had lasted only three minutes. The frightened household clustered at the top of the stairway. From below, as from a deep, black emptiness, came a gurgling sound, as of air bubbling through water. Sometimes this gurgle changed to a sound almost like a whistle. But this, too, quickly died down. Then nothing came up out of the blackness except the heavy panting of some creature struggling mightily for air.

Weedon Scott pressed a button, and the staircase and downstairs hall were flooded with light. Then he and Judge Scott, revolvers in hand, cautiously descended. There was no need for this caution. White Fang had done his work. In the midst of the wreckage of overthrown and smashed furniture, partly on his side, his face hidden by an arm, lay a man. Weedon Scott bent over, removed the arm, and turned the man's face upward. A gaping throat explained the manner of his death.

"Jim Hall," said Judge Scott, and father and son looked significantly at each other.

Then they turned to White Fang. He, too, was lying on his side. His eyes were closed, but the lids slightly lifted in an effort to look at them as they bent over him. The tail twitched in a vain effort to wag. Weedon Scott patted him, and White Fang's throat rumbled an acknowledging growl. But it was a weak growl at best, and it quickly ceased. His eyelids drooped and went shut, and his whole body seemed to relax and flatten out upon the floor.

"He's done for, poor devil," muttered the master.

"We'll see about that," asserted the Judge, starting for the telephone. The country doctor was soon on his way in great haste.

"Frankly, he has one chance in a thousand," announced the doctor, after he had worked an hour and a half on White Fang. Dawn was breaking through the windows and dimming the electric lights. Except for the children, the whole family was gathered about to hear the medical verdict.

"One broken hind leg," he went on. "Three broken ribs, and at least one has pierced the lungs. He has lost nearly all the blood in his body. Most likely, he also has internal injuries. He must have been jumped upon. There are also three bullet holes clear through him. One chance in a thousand is too much to hope for. He doesn't have even one chance in ten thousand."

"But he mustn't lose any chance for survival," Judge Scott exclaimed. "Never mind the expense. Put him under the X-ray—do whatever it takes. Weedon, telegraph at once to San Francisco for Doctor Nichols. No offense intended, Doctor, but he must have every chance we can give him."

The doctor smiled indulgently. "Of course I understand. He deserves all that can be done for him. He must be nursed as you would nurse a sick child. And be sure to watch his temperature. I'll be back again at ten o'clock."

White Fang was indeed nursed. Judge Scott's suggestion of a trained nurse was noisily and indignantly vetoed by the girls, who undertook the job themselves. And White Fang won out on the one chance in ten thousand.

The doctor had good reasons for giving

White Fang such low odds. All his adult life the doctor had tended and operated on soft, civilized humans, who lived sheltered lives and descended from many sheltered generations. Compared with White Fang, they were frail and flabby, and they clutched life weakly. White Fang had come straight from the Wild, where the weak perish early and no place is completely safe. In neither his father nor his mother was there any weakness, nor was there any in the generations before them. An inner will of iron and the vital health of the Wild were White Fang's inheritance. Every part of him clung to life with the tenacity that once belonged to all creatures.

Encased in the plaster casts and bandages, White Fang lingered for weeks. He slept long hours and dreamed much, and through his mind passed an unending display of Northland visions. All the ghosts of the past arose and were with him. Once again he lived in the lair with Kiche, crept trembling to the knees of Gray Beaver to offer his allegiance, ran for his life before Lip-lip and all the howling bedlam of the puppy-pack.

He ran again through the silence, hunting his living food through the months of famine. Again he ran at the head of the team, the gut-whips of Mit-sah and Gray Beaver snapping behind, their voices crying, *"Raa! Raa!"* when they came to a narrow passage and the team closed together like a fan to go through it. He relived all his days with Beauty Smith and the fights he had fought. At such times he whimpered and snarled in his sleep, and those watching him said that he was having bad dreams.

But there was one particular nightmare from which he suffered—the clanking, clanging monsters of electric street cars that seemed to him like colossal screaming lynxes. He would lie in a screen of bushes, watching for a squirrel to venture far enough out on the ground from its tree-refuge. Then, when he sprang out upon it, it would transform itself into a street car, towering over him like a mountain, screaming and clanging and spitting fire at him. It was the same when he challenged the hawk down out of the sky. It would rush down out of the blue on him, changing itself into the infernal street car. Or again, he would be in the pen of Beauty Smith. Outside the pen, men would be gathering, and he knew that a fight was on. He watched the door for his enemy to enter. The door would open, and thrust in upon him would be the awful street car. This occurred a thousand times, and each time the terror it inspired was as vivid and great as ever.

Then came the day—a day of celebration—when the last bandage and the last plaster cast were taken off. All Sierra Vista was gathered around. The master rubbed his ears, and White Fang crooned his love-growl. The master's wife called him the "Blessed Wolf," and all the women began to call him by this name.

He tried to rise to his feet, but after several attempts fell down from weakness. He had been lying down so long that his muscles had grown weak. He felt a little shame because of his weakness, as though he were failing in his service to the gods. In his embarrassment, he made a heroic effort to arise. At last he stood on his four legs, tottering and swaying back and forth.

"The Blessed Wolf!" chorused the women.

Judge Scott surveyed them triumphantly.

"You finally admit it with your own mouths," he said. "Just as I claimed right along. No mere dog could have done what he did. He's a wolf."

"A Blessed Wolf," corrected the Judge's wife.

"Yes, Blessed Wolf," agreed the Judge. "And from now on that shall be my name for him."

"He'll have to learn to walk again," said the doctor. "So he might as well start right now. It won't hurt him. Take him outside."

And outside he went, like a king, with all Sierra Vista as his court. He was very weak, and when he reached the lawn he lay down and rested for a while.

Then the procession continued, with little spurts of strength coming into White Fang's muscles as the blood began to surge through them. He reached the stables, and there in the doorway lay Collie, a half-dozen pudgy puppies playing about her in the sun.

White Fang looked on with a wondering eye. Collie snarled warningly at him, and he was careful to keep his distance. With a toe, the master helped one sprawling puppy come toward him. He bristled suspiciously, but the master's actions told him that all was well. Collie, held in the arms of one of the women, watched him jealously. Her snarl warned him clearly that all was not well.

The puppy sprawled in front of him. He cocked his ears and watched it curiously. Then their noses touched, and he felt the warm little tongue of the puppy on his jowl. With no idea why, White Fang's tongue went out, and he licked the puppy's face.

Hand-clapping and pleased cries from the

gods greeted the performance. White Fang was surprised and looked at them in puzzlement. Then his weakness won out, and he lay down, his ears cocked, his head on one side, as he watched the puppy. To Collie's great disgust, the other puppies came sprawling toward him, and he gravely permitted them to climb and tumble over him. At first, amid the applause of the gods, he showed a trifle of his old self-consciousness and awkwardness. This passed away as the puppies' antics and mauling continued, and he lay with half-shut, patient eyes, drowsing in the sun.

AFTERWORD
by Beth Johnson

Suppose that three people who had read this novel were asked, "What's *White Fang* about?" The first might simply say, "It's about the life of a wolf-dog." The second might answer, "It's about how people and animals lived in the frozen North a hundred years ago." From the third you might hear, "It's basically a story about cruelty versus kindness."

These three different responses make an important point about studying literature. Literature is not an exact science, like math. Imagine asking someone to divide 45 by 9. If the person answers 5, he is correct. If he answers anything else, he is incorrect. That's not how the study of literature works. Sure, there are questions that have "right" and "wrong" answers, but they are generally questions about facts. Examples of such questions include, "Who were White Fang's parents?" or "Why did Jim Hall break into Weedon Scott's house?"

But much of the pleasure of studying literature comes from the fact that it is *not* an exact science. Each person who reads *White Fang* (or any story) comes to it from a different perspective, or point of view. Your own unique perspective affects what you notice in the story, how you respond to it, and what conclusions you draw from it. From that perspective, you can develop your own theories about what the book is about and what messages are hidden beneath its surface. Just as Jack London performed a creative act in writing *White Fang*, you, the reader, can be creative in your response to it. This is literary analysis, and the only limitation placed on you as you perform it is this: You must back up your opinions with solid evidence from the book. If you are able to do that, you are as qualified to analyze *White Fang*, or any other piece of literature, as any university professor.

What does all this add up to? It's simply this: There is no one way to study *White Fang*. There are dozens, even hundreds of ways to explore, enjoy, and understand it. Just to get your own exploration started, however, let's look at several of the important themes that London has woven through the novel.

One of those themes is "survival of the fittest." This is an idea that was receiving a great deal of attention in 1906, the year of *White Fang's* publication. It had been introduced by Charles Darwin, a British scientist. Darwin had concluded that animal species change, or evolve, slowly over thousands of years. Such change, he said, came about through a process called "natural selection." What Darwin meant was this: Animals produce many more offspring than are needed to replace the parents. The earth can't support all these creatures, so they must compete for food and shelter. The animals that are "fittest"—that is, best equipped for survival— tend to live to adulthood and reproduce, while the less fit animals don't survive long enough to reproduce. Therefore, those fit animals are "selected" by nature to pass on their genetic traits to the next generation.

Darwin's ideas were very controversial, especially among people who thought that "natural selection" contradicted the idea that God alone was in control of the universe. But London's own life on the rough streets of Oakland, pirating in San Francisco Bay, and traveling as a hobo had convinced him that in this world, only the strong survive. His belief was strengthened during his time as a gold prospector in Alaska and Canada, where he lived in close contact with nature. He poured this belief into his depiction of White Fang and the wolf-dog's struggle through life.

White Fang, you remember, is the only one of his litter to survive puppyhood. Food is scarce, and three of the original five have died. Only White Fang and one sister remains. Then One Eye, their father, shows up with a porcupine he had killed. "[White Fang's] little body rounded out with the meat he now ate, but the food had come too late for her. Reduced to a skeleton wrapped in skin, she slept until the flame of her life flickered and died out." Already it is apparent that White Fang is somehow tougher, stronger, and better equipped for survival than others of his kind.

In the next few months, as White Fang ventures out from the cave where he was born, he further demonstrates that he is well suited for survival. When he stumbles into a nest of baby birds, he promptly kills and eats them. He finds an orphan baby weasel and kills and eats that. He does not feel sorry for the weaker creatures that he kills, or wonder if it is right for him to live by killing them.

As White Fang grows to maturity, his fitness for survival is illustrated on nearly every page. Not only is he a large, powerful animal, but he has an unusual trait that gives him an advantage in fights. Unlike most dogs, who bristle, growl, and circle before an attack, White Fang attacks without warning. He will kill another of his own species as quickly—and coldly—as he will kill a rabbit for his supper. This willingness to fight, and the fear of him that other dogs develop as a result, helps to ensure his survival.

In the end, of course, every fighter meets his match. If he had lived out his life in the wild North, chances are that White Fang would finally have run into a younger, quicker version of himself. Nature doesn't play favorites: as soon as such an opponent had come along, White Fang himself would have been killed. But because he survives long enough to be adopted into a loving home, White Fang has the prospect of a peaceful, easy old age. He can nap in the sun at Weedon Scott's farm, father many litters of puppies, and pass on his superior traits to them.

A second important theme in *White Fang* is the idea that while hate creates hate, love creates love. Throughout most of the book, White Fang is anything but a lovable character. He is cruel, aggressive, grouchy, and solitary. But London suggests that White Fang wasn't born mean; he has grown mean for a reason. As a little puppy, he had cheerfully played with his brothers and sisters, and he had felt deep love for his mother. But once he and his mother, Kiche, are taken to the Indian camp, White Fang's troubles begin. He is beaten into obedience by his master, Gray Beaver. Even worse, he is targeted for abuse by Lip-lip, a bully of a puppy. The other puppies in the camp follow Lip-lip's example and make White Fang's life miserable. Understandably, he develops a deep hatred for other dogs which lasts for many years.

As White Fang becomes an adult, he is exposed to more cruelty, which leads to his becoming an even more hate-filled animal. Gray Beaver trades the dog to Beauty Smith, a truly evil human being. His new owner confines White Fang to a cage and forces him to fight other animals to the death for money. He allows men to torment the dog, poking him with sticks while he rages inside his cell. Beauty laughs with delight as he sees White Fang become, in London's words, "a fiend."

But according to London, just as hate has the power to create hate, love can create love. Love comes into White Fang's life in the form of Weedon Scott, a young mining expert. Scott rescues White Fang from a dogfight that almost surely would have killed him. Afterwards, Scott gently and patiently works to win White Fang's trust. He take the chain off White Fang, allowing him his first freedom for a long time. He talks to him in a soft, kind voice. He gives him meat, and he does not punish him when White Fang bites him and kills another dog that tries to rob him of his food. Eventually White Fang accepts a piece of meat from Scott's hand and even allows Scott to pet him.

Scott's kindly touch sets off an amazing transformation within White Fang. In London's words, "To change now was to tear down and rebuild the habits of a lifetime. And yet Weedon Scott had the power to remold him."

At first, White Fang only *likes* this new human master. But when Scott goes away on a business trip, White Fang misses him so deeply that he becomes sick. He refuses to eat, allows the other dogs to bully him, and is near death when Scott returns home. From that point on, it is clear that White Fang's *love* for Scott is the most important thing in his life. This love is so profound that White Fang is able to adjust to a completely different way of life with his master.

On a California farm, he learns to tolerate and even like Scott's parents, wife, and children. Most surprisingly of all, he also learns to live in harmony with the farm's other animals. His mating with Collie, the farm's sheepdog, and gentle treatment of their puppies is final evidence that love has overcome the power of hate within him.

These are only two of the many themes waiting to be discovered in *White Fang*. One final word about the novel and its author, Jack London: In *White Fang*, London tells the story of a wolf-dog born wild, but forced by circumstances to grow up among human beings. London was so interested in the relationship between humans and dogs, and in the themes of nature and survival, that he wrote a book describing a dog who went through the opposite process. That book, *The Call of the Wild*, is about Buck, a pet dog who is kidnapped and forced to learn to live as a wild animal. It is a very different story, and a fascinating one to compare to *White Fang*. If you enjoyed this book and have not yet read *The Call of the Wild*, you have another wonderful dog story to experience.